"What's the matter, darling, your control of the situation slipping?"

"Get out!" she yelled. Her rage was barely contained.

He brought his face down to hers and, nose to nose, shaped his throaty words with a white flash of hard teeth and a ruthless mouth.

"Make me."

"Oh, no." She gave him a malicious smile. "You haven't got what it takes to drive me *that* far out of control."

"That sounds remarkably like a challenge," Matt purred, his hazel eyes fierce.

AMANDA CARPENTER, who wrote her first Harlequin romance when she was nineteen, was raised in South Bend, Indiana. She now lives in England, where she endeavors to enhance the quality of her romance novels with original story lines and an individual style. When she's not writing, Amanda pursues interests in art, music and fashion.

Books by Amanda Carpenter

HARLEQUIN PRESENTS
991—ROSE-COLOURED LOVE
1047—RECKLESS
1127—THE GIFT OF HAPPINESS
1175—CAPRICE
1384—PASSAGE OF THE NIGHT
1596—CRY WOLF

HARLEQUIN ROMANCE
2605—A DEEPER DIMENSION
2648—A DAMAGED TRUST

AMANDA CARPENTER

A Solitary Heart

Harlequin Books

TORONTO • NEW YORK • LONDON
AMSTERDAM • PARIS • SYDNEY • HAMBURG
STOCKHOLM • ATHENS • TOKYO • MILAN
MADRID • WARSAW • BUDAPEST • AUCKLAND

ISBN 0-373-11635-7

A SOLITARY HEART

CHAPTER ONE

WHO was he?

The question, intimate as only a thought that would never be divulged could be, ran through her mind as she surreptitiously watched the man who had just appeared on the back porch.

His presence had certainly made a forceful impact, and not just on her. People looked. They, like Sian, couldn't help themselves, for the man was hard angles and sheathed intent, white-shirted and haloed in golden sunshine and quite staggeringly beautiful for a man, beautiful in the way of a lean, hungry cat. In one hand he held a sweating beer can, powerful fingers negligently gentle on the aluminium, and with the other he pushed back the tawny hair from his forehead.

Sian took a sip of her chilled wine, smiling to herself as loud guffaws burst from a nearby group. She had taken a moment from socialising to lean against a tree-trunk, grateful for the shade in the heat of the day.

She and her room-mate, Jane, were born just a week apart, and were having a combined birthday, Memorial Day and graduation celebration. They had just completed their senior year of final exams at Notre Dame University, and all their university friends, families and friends of the families had been invited to the party.

The idea had been a simple one a few months ago, but somewhere along in the planning it had grown into monstrous proportions, until Sian felt it wise to invite all their neighbours as well. Best to make allies from potential opposition, then nobody could complain about the noise. More than a hundred people milled about the ground-floor apartment and spilled out on to the wide back lawn. It was a crushing, noisy crowd in eighty-five-degree weather. Guests had started to arrive at noon that Sunday, and at four o'clock everyone was relaxed and convivial.

The man stepped off the porch, and his torso was framed in light, from the tight hip to the tough broad shoulders.

Sian wasn't surprised that she didn't know him. She was only acquainted with about a third of the people at the party. His connection was probably tenuous at best: a friend of a friend, a second cousin of a neighbour. If he could be anything as mundane as that.

One sweep from a dark gaze spanned the group, and he began to prowl.

The raw grace of his body made her mouth grow dry. He was masculinity in expression, fluidity in aggressive motion, a predator lazily casing the herd.

How many men at the party? How many men had she met throughout her life, of all shapes and ages and sizes? They were a parade of pale imitations to this luminous reality. Once she had thought differently, but now she knew that she had never known the definition of a man before. Sian struggled to hide her crazy heartbeat and trembling hands under her customary cool poise.

His eyes locked with hers.

He strode towards her.

Sian jerked her gaze away, a tell-tale reaction eloquent with rejection. It was a delusion. It had to be. The stranger was a devil to climb inside her head so, but he couldn't possibly live up to the promise of his first impression. He would open his mouth and utter something banal, and the spell would be shattered. In a moment she would breathe normally, and her world would be sane again. The roaring silence that filled her mind would resolve into babble, loud music and the civilised enjoyment of good friends sharing a moment of triumph together. This wild thing invading her would pass unnoticed into oblivion.

Then Lucifer, morning star, the brightest and the most beautiful of all the archangels, appeared slowly through the smoky swirl blown off the barbecue, and halted in front of her.

She could not ignore him, and must not pretend to. Her heavy green eyes lifted from contemplating her glass of wine. The stranger's face was hard, uncompromising, his sardonic hazel eyes two quartz chips honed to razor-sharpness.

Here it comes. Something trite and meaningless, she prayed. What's a nice girl like you...?

'Sian Riley?'

The fluid voice that would be velvet in tenderness now grated on her hypersensitive hearing.

Her expression was closed to the observer, the lovely features locked as tight as a treasure vault. 'Yes?' she replied, amazed at the calm in her reply. 'What can I do for you?'

His predator's eyes raked her, claws naked and judgemental. He said, soft and tight and ungentle, 'Just one thing, Ms Riley. My name is Matthew Severn, and I want you to stay away from my brother Joshua.'

'What?' Sian gasped, any possible comprehension of their meeting blown to smithereens by those gunshot words. She leaned more heavily against the tree-trunk, her incredulous gaze telling the man confronting her that he was a madman.

'You heard what I said.' The stranger lifted his hand, and for one awful moment, as her shocked eyes watched it come towards her face, Sian thought he meant to slap her.

She couldn't move. The strong, graceful hand went to the tree-trunk behind her head, and he leaned the weight of his body into his powerful outstretched arm. Corded muscle in his bicep flexed with tension, a small shift under the sleeve of the white shirt, as he trapped her into intimate confrontation with his body and his undiluted antagonism.

'Joshua Severn,' he growled very quietly. 'My brother. Your fiancé. Stay away from him, Ms Riley. This is the only warning you'll get. You're not his kind.'

Somewhere Sian had stepped, all unsuspecting, through some invisible barrier into an incomprehensible nightmare. Her green eyes seemed to collect jagged shards of illumination into coalesced rage.

'How dare you?' she said from the back of her throat, still reeling internally from the unexpected assault. The stranger's proximity was an intimidation she refused to knuckle under. She leaned forward from the waist and glared up at him. 'Just who the *hell* do you think you are?'

'As trustee in control of Josh's inheritance, I'm a man in a position of some authority,' Matthew Severn replied silkenly. 'And I assure you, I shall exercise that authority to the limit. You're not acceptable partnership material and, whatever advantages you might think to acquire from marrying Joshua, you can forget it. I'll make sure he doesn't see a cent before his thirtieth birthday. You'll both face years of struggle to get through graduate school, so wise up now. This isn't Easy Street.'

'No,' Sian agreed in a snarl, transformed from the porcelain grace of her former repose into a tempestuous, vitalising fury. 'This isn't Easy Street. This is my home, and you've just violated all the rules of courteous conduct by your boorish intrusive manner and your insane allegations! I want you to get out now!'

'How convenient that would make things for you, wouldn't it? Well, I have no intention of leaving until this is resolved!' Matthew snapped, then ran his gaze down the length of her body compulsively. 'Look at you—butter wouldn't melt in your mouth until somebody crosses you, then all hell breaks loose. What's the matter, darling, your control of the situation slipping?'

'Get out!' she snarled, for he was quite right. Her rage was out of control.

He brought his face down to hers and, nose to nose, shaped his throaty words with a white flash of hard teeth and a ruthless mouth. 'Make me.'

Sian felt a flicker of insight and clutched at it. He was too taunting, too provocative. How he would love for her to cause a scene in front of everyone. Her green eyes narrowed, the raven slant of her sleek brows pronounced. 'Oh, no,' she said gently, and gave him a malicious smile. 'You haven't got what it takes to drive me that far out of control.'

'Young lady,' he purred, the angles of his face taut and breathtaking, those hazel eyes fierce, 'that sounds remarkably like a challenge.'

Sian's whole being was a weapon, as she replied breathily, 'What a concept! Who could presume to challenge the opinions of one such as you? By his own account, a man in a position of some authority!'

'Who indeed?' he agreed, in that soft, velvet and steel voice. 'One would think only pyromaniacs would be so foolish.'

'While only insecure little men feel the need to prove themselves,' she shot back, quick as a striking snake. If anything his hot gaze grew even hotter, and his tiny smile should have warned her.

'Prove themselves in what area, Sian Riley?' he murmured mockingly. Those hot eyes dropped, to the racing pulsemark in her creamy throat, to her breasts. 'Prove themselves how many times, and in what—position?'

Another woman might have recoiled from the sexual innuendo in distaste or confusion, but she saw that it was what he expected, and another wave of anger washed over her. She snapped nastily, 'I would think you're just the type to know all about untenable positions!'

That had his roving gaze springing back to her angry expression in amazement, then, to her astonishment, he threw back his tawny head and laughed out loud. It came from his chest, free and infectiously generous. Sian was encased in ice, however, and was not tempted.

'Darling,' he drawled in lazy amusement, 'there's nothing untenable about my positions.'

'You would think so.' She matched him blow for blow, only her amusement was cold and pitying. 'Personally, I'm unimpressed. I never did see the attraction of a legend in one's own mind.'

She would have slipped away then, but his other hand dropped the empty beer can and shot to hold her, and the shocking contact of his warm long fingers curling around her bare arm made her teeth clash together.

'No,' he said, his face dark and satiric, 'you prefer younger men who are easily influenced by all the wrong things. Tell me, does Joshua know what a temper you have? Has he ever borne the brunt of your sharp tongue?'

This man was making her crazy. His confrontational, abrasive attitude, his accusations, his warm touch on her sensitive skin, his very presence—Sian felt goaded beyond endurance. She gritted, reactive and rash, 'I guarantee that Joshua doesn't find my tongue sharp at all.'

She heard his breathing halt as suddenly as if she'd knifed him; over the noise and tumult of the party, she heard it. Or perhaps she had felt it, through the searing physical connection. Or perhaps she had imagined it, for his face was stone. She couldn't endure being so close to him any more and tried to wrench away, but his fingers tightened convulsively.

Matthew Severn said, with terrible simplicity and conviction, 'My brother is not the man for you. Accept it, Sian.'

Out of the corner of her eye, she saw two of her former class-mates coming towards them, their expressions insupportably cheerful, their eyes avidly curious. On Matthew, eating him alive. She stiffened, and said to him with cold courtesy, 'Your reiteration is noted. I see you've finished your drink. Why don't I get you another?'

Even as she became the gracious hostess, Matthew saw the approaching pair, and his hold on her arm dropped away as he adopted the role of polite guest so smoothly that she stared in consternation. His charm was absolutely seamless, and deadly as the edge of a cliff. She hated him quite passionately.

'Don't bother, I can help myself,' he said, and gave her a remarkably beautiful public smile as he added privately, 'This isn't over.'

'What a pretentious creature you are; of course it is,' murmured Sian in a fine show of contemptuous indifference as she stepped away.

Matthew engaged the other two women in light conversation, ignoring her as if she didn't exist. Trite and meaningless phrases, and they snapped it up.

Sian's expression was very dry. The heel of her narrow, elegant shoe knocked something and she looked down. After a moment, she bent and picked up the beer can. It was crushed almost beyond recognition.

Sian held on to her composure by sheer force of will until she finally managed to escape to the study. She shut the door on any possible prying eyes, collapsed weakly into the chair pulled back from her desk and dropped her face into one unsteady hand. A flashback to the unpleasant little scene in the back garden made her jaw harden and her eyes blaze anew.

How *dared* Matt Severn speak to her like that? How *dared* he look down his aquiline nose at her with such contempt? She'd seen that look before, on others who thought they were better than she because of her chequered past and disreputable family.

Sian was proud of all the things she had seen and done as a child. Her mother had died when she was too young to really remember her, and so she had tagged along on Devin Riley's travels and entered a carnival world of famous places and people. Regarded through a child's innocent eyes, it had been a fabulous life. Rio de Janeiro, Monte Carlo, London, Rome, Las Vegas—Sian had seen them all before she was ten, and her father, heart-wrenchingly handsome and charming as the sun was bright, with a computer brain and a gilded tongue, had seemed like a fairy-tale prince who walked a higher plane of existence from other mere mortals.

It was only when she was old enough to be sent away to boarding school that Sian grew to realise just how flamboyant and bizarre her childhood had really been. Before the whispers and the gossip that had interrupted many a budding friendship, she had merely accepted the lifestyle as normal. That was how Devin lived. He loved her, but men with his particular glamour and genius couldn't be expected to settle down in one place just for a little girl who missed her daddy when he left her all alone in a strange place.

Sian smiled that wry twist of the mouth that so characterised her pensive turn of thought. She was indeed her father's daughter. After the first year or so of loneliness and bewilderment, she had got the measure of all those whispering gossips and proceeded to charm them one by one, those songbirds in the bushes, until they were eating out of her hand. Her school years had been, in the main, positive after that and, during the holidays when she was not travelling with her father, she was visiting at the homes of her friends.

She had been happy—oh, yes—and she wouldn't trade her colourful memories for anything. Her father Devin could still steal the heart of the devil, who would thank him for the pleasure, and she loved to see him when he made the rare visit.

But something had happened to the little girl who'd begged for more champagne with her breakfast. Either the schools had taught her otherwise, or Sian had grown up to realise it for herself. Whatever the reason, however the cause, she had a deep, abiding yearning for a solid, secure life.

Sian had a middle-class mentality. She wanted a home, family, a steady job, the same circle of friends that she could relate to and grow older with. She wanted to belong, somewhere, somehow. If anyone had asked her what her goals were, that would be her first reply. She wouldn't even think to wonder, in that first instant of reaction, if they might have been asking about something so obvious as a choice of career.

And if it was one thing guaranteed to drive her absolutely wild, beyond any hope or shade of reason, it was to come up against narrow-minded bigots like Matt Severn! One sneer got past all her guards; one judgemental opinion breached all her defences. He, a total stranger, had hurt her today, as she stood marble-faced and icy, then hot with eruptive anger by turns before him, and it wasn't any use to realise afterwards just how ridiculous his behaviour had been. He had got right inside, and Sian did not forgive easily.

Sian swivelled in her chair and reached automatically into the top drawer of the desk.

The door to the study opened some ten minutes later, and she looked up. Her room-mate Jane slid inside and shut the door behind her. Noise from the party blared loudly, then resumed the muted musical beat that carried through the floorboards and pounded in the walls.

'Hey, Solitaire,' said her bubbly friend. 'What are you doing in here all by yourself? We've food and drink and a whole army to feed off it outside!'

Sian smiled at Jane. 'I'm just catching a moment of peace and relative quiet.'

'Right,' said Jane, as she settled like a fluffy cat on one corner of the desk they'd shared for four years, 'speak to me, woman. You're young, gorgeous, and supremely talented as a budding dress designer, and you've just sailed through your undergraduate finals. What's more, you've got hunky Joshua Severn panting like a lovesick puppy at your heels. So what gives?'

Sian had smiled reluctantly at Jane's brisk, no-nonsense recital of her worldly assets, but at the mention of Joshua's name her expression had darkened. She puckered her mouth into a delicate peach rosebud and prevaricated, 'Why does anything have to "give"? Can't I want to be by myself for a few moments?'

'Sian, you're my best friend and I quite love you to distraction,' replied Jane in a light tone that belied her shrewd gaze, 'and I do mean distraction. You always play solitaire when you're troubled. Always. Obsessively. Game after game after game, so don't try to pull the wool over my eyes! I want to know what's going on and why you're sitting alone in a shadowed room on a beautiful sunny day.'

Sian sighed and immediately wished it hadn't come out sounding quite so heavy, and she busied herself with sweeping the cards expertly into one hand. Then, as if her shapely fingers had acquired a mind of their own, they commenced shuffling and reshuffling the pack. Jane watched with admiration the manoeuvres that were as slick and polished as a professional croupier's, another legacy from Sian's father.

'Nothing's wrong,' she insisted. Jane's glance turned into a glare. 'Honestly, nothing's *wrong*. It's just that— Joshua's older brother Matt is out there.'

'Whew!' Jane wiped her brow in an exaggerated expression of relief. 'And here I thought you hadn't even noticed the sexiest, most virile, exciting man present! There for a moment you had me worried! Aren't you a cool customer?'

'Not exactly,' said Sian with a delicate bite, and her right hand splayed the deck of cards into a fan and snapped them shut. 'Not—quite—exactly. Mr Matthew Severn condescended to notice me upon his unexpected arrival and made sure to communicate in precise terms just how unsuitable I was in the role of Joshua's future wife. I was a fortune-hunter and Joshua a victim, and he would make our lives hell were we to go through with the marriage. Et cetera, et cetera.'

'*What*?' It was not so much a question as a high shriek of astonishment, and Jane fell off the desk and into her lap, gabbling. 'You sly dog! When did Joshua propose, for heaven's sake? And what did you tell him? How dare you keep this a secret from me?'

'That,' said Sian coldly with hot, glittering eyes as she wrapped both arms around the other girl in an instinctive gesture to keep her from falling to the floor, 'is the crux of the matter. Joshua hasn't asked me yet. He probably hasn't got up the courage to, poor boy. The very first *I* heard of this was from the devil himself. Accompanied, of course, with a thorough lashing from those go-to-hell eyes.'

'Oh, no!' Jane stuffed the heel of one hand into her mouth, staring over it at her, eyes wide and scandalised. 'And you with a temper as hot and as Irish as they come—what did you do?'

Reel from shock, ache inside, feel buffeted like a gale-blown leaf. Janey, Janey, there weren't enough words. Sian gritted from between bared white teeth, 'I called him boorish and intrusive and pretentious.'

'Aha, that's my girl!' Jane threw her arms around Sian for an exuberant hug. 'And what did he do?'

Sian buried her face into her friend's slim shoulder and began to shake with fury and laughter. 'You don't want to know! Jane, that's why Joshua has been wandering around looking so whipped and worried. He's been trying to corner me all day. I don't know what to say to him if he asks me. If he'd caught me when I was really angry, I might have said yes just for spite!'

'Would you want to say yes anyway—for your sake, not for Joshua's or Matt's?' asked Jane, sobering.

Sian groaned, long and low and full of frustration. 'God, I don't know! Joshua's so sweet and gentle, considerate and handsome. What's more he'd be the ideal husband and father——'

Jane slipped off her lap and on to the floor, leaning against her knees. 'But,' she said gently, 'what about love?'

'Love!' Sian used the word like an expletive, a furious snort of contempt with a curl of her lip and flashing, brilliant eyes. To her watching and concerned friend, she was magnificent and all woman, her lustrous raven hair spilling like midnight down the ivory cream of a willowy neck and shoulders, a creature of high spirit and sensuality who was totally oblivious to the fact. 'What did love get my mother? A thoroughly enchanting ne'er-do-well, a handsome faithless lover with wanderlust and the gambling itch—don't get me wrong, I love my father too. That's precisely why I think so little of the emotion. Love, Janey, darling, is not on my list of requirements. Stability, constancy, devotion—they're what's important and Joshua could be the man to give them to me. I just don't know.'

'Oh, Sian.' Jane sighed and pressed her hands.

The dim, far-away look in Sian's gaze sharpened slowly to the present awareness and she looked down at the blonde's upturned face. What was Jane's expression?

Love, a dear certainty—tinged with a hint of sadness and . . . pity?

She felt shocked at the prospect, quite failing to see why she should be pitied, unless it was for having undergone such a humiliating, infuriating encounter on what was meant to be a day of sharing and celebration.

'Well,' she said briskly, with a glint in her eye as she shook off her reverie, 'what about joining this party, then?'

'That's my girl!' said Jane, who scrambled to her feet and straightened her dishevelled dress. They made a perfect foil for each other, one small and sun-kissed brown with light golden hair, the other tall with raven hair and creamy skin.

'I'd murder to have legs like yours!' exclaimed Jane ruefully. 'I can't think how Joshua's brother managed to be so hateful instead of eating you up! You're a killer in that red dress—if I wore something like that, the dropped waist would be down around my knees! It's a wonder he didn't throw you over his shoulder and make off with you the moment he laid eyes on you!'

'Somehow,' said Sian very drily, 'he managed to contain himself. Not that you find me weeping with disappointment. My other reactions are far too satisfying for that!'

Her room-mate hesitated in the act of striding out of the door and looked at her sharply, then began to smile. 'Why, I declare, Solitaire, you've got a devil twinkling out of your eye. Just what do you have fermenting in your nasty little mind?'

'Not a lot,' she purred sweetly as her anger settled cold and wicked in the pit of her stomach. 'But if Matt is so determined to consider me unsuitable for his august, respectable family, I might have to show him just how unsuitable I can be.'

'Do count me in,' whispered Jane delightedly. 'That bad old sexy man can't tell *my* best friend off and get away with it! What are you going to do?'

She shrugged. 'Play it by ear. After all, he's already declared war. I'll just wave the red flag around and see what happens.'

She followed Jane out of the room and down the short hall to the kitchen, and then there was no more time for intimate conversation, for they were engulfed in light, and noise and the welcoming cries from their friends.

Instantly upon entering the kitchen, Sian felt the heat of attention radiating from the man in the corner. Her betraying gaze winged over to him; yes, she had not been mistaken. By some radar sense she managed to pin-point where he was.

Matt Severn was leaning against a low open window-sill beside Joshua, appearing to talk to the parents of Jane's boyfriend Steven, who lived in Michigan City and had come to South Bend for the day.

The hunter appeared to be at ease, but Sian took in a silent quivering breath under the weight of his sharp stabbing stare. Why did this have to be so difficult? Why did he have to look at her in such an appraising, antagonistic way? Why did she have to feel so intimidated and somehow *small* for all her height of five feet ten?

He was too hard; not stone-cold hard, but the healthy, aggressive hardness of sophistication, maturity and physical confidence, and by comparison with the impact of his presence she felt a frailty in the curvature of her bones and slim body in a way she'd never felt before.

Then Joshua strolled over and put his arm casually around her shoulders, and Sian saw Matt Severn's gaze shift infinitesimally at the movement, and his subtle, inward calculation, and all her self-confidence came surging back. She gave him an insouciant smile and saw him register that as well with dark anger, and then she turned her attention to Joshua.

'Happy birthday, beautiful,' said Joshua with a grin. 'What have you been up to?'

'No good; you can bet on it,' she replied as she slipped her arm around his waist, and she coaxed his beer from him to take a quick sip. That looked intimate, didn't it, Matt? Eat that until you choke on it.

'Cake time!' called out Steven. Jane clapped her hands, eyes glowing, and a frothy confection appeared that had Jane's and Sian's names written on the top. It was ablaze with candles. After the cake came presents, and wine, and the last of the afternoon flitted away.

People moved in and out of the apartment, danced outside in the back yard, cooked hamburgers and hot dogs and drank beer. Sian slipped away from the group in the kitchen and went to get some supper. The sun was setting, the breeze turning cool at last, and, though a few of the older folk had left already, the party was still in full swing. It looked as if it might carry on all night and, since the next day was a holiday, probably would.

As she was piling coleslaw and potato salad on to a paper plate, Joshua sidled up to her, and Sian sighed with resignation. Masking her irritation, for she didn't feel up to handling a tête-à-tête with him at the moment, she smiled at him and said, 'Be a love and get me a glass of wine, will you? My throat is parched after talking so much.'

He planted a kiss on the tip of her nose. 'Don't go off dancing with somebody while I'm gone.'

'That'd be a trick,' she muttered as she looked down at her laden plate, even as Joshua left her side. 'I'd end up putting coleslaw down their front.'

'Putting coleslaw down whose front?'

The lazy voice came from her other side and a curling thread of anger trickled hot fingers down her spine as her head jerked in surprise. She had dared to hope that Matt would go with the other early departures, for he lived in Chicago, which was a good two-hour drive away, but he had hung around instead. Spying on her the whole time, if his prompt appearance was anything to go by.

She squelched the traitorous gratitude that she was, at least, spared any intimacy with his younger brother and managed to find a dry, even tone. 'There are possibilities. What a good attention span you have. Do you like what you see?'

And she could have immediately bitten her wayward tongue out as Matt ran his predator's eyes down her entire length—heavens, he had to be well over six feet tall—and said, with mocking amusement, 'Drop-dead legs and a pretty smile. I've got to hand it to the little brother—he's got good aesthetics.'

Sian's paper plate trembled and she gripped it so hard in an effort to steady herself that she buckled the edges. But her face remained smooth; she even managed to wrinkle her nose in faint distaste. 'I don't know; the description sounds vaguely heavy metal to me. I'm surprised. I would have thought your tastes ran to the more conservative.'

The setting sun slanted across his hard, intent face, and for the merest instant those hazel eyes were lit and reflective. The effect was barbaric, uncanny. He almost didn't look human. Sian fought the urge to step back in alarm. He said, soft and gentle, 'But we weren't talking about my tastes, just my brother's.'

'What about your brother?' asked Joshua, reappearing at her side with her wine and a newly opened beer. He looked defiant as he challenged Matt's presence, and almost childishly unformed next to the other man's chiselled, hard features.

Sian consigned yet another sigh to the nether regions of her empty stomach. It looked to all intents and purposes as if the two men would wrangle over her right then and there like two dogs over a bone, never mind what the bone thought of the contention. The situation was passing beyond the ridiculous into the farcical.

'Oh, you got it, thanks,' she said with outward poise to Joshua and took the wine. 'We were just discussing individual tastes. I said Matt seemed the conservative type.'

Joshua laughed rather too loudly. 'Matt's about as conservative as a race-track. What he got up to in *his* youth shouldn't be told in polite company.'

One corner of Matt's sensually cut lips pulled to the side, and what were engaging dimples in Joshua's young handsome face were deep creases stamped into his older brother, signs of decision, temper, and, yes, humour. The two looked alike only in their colouring and general build of body, and, when they were standing side by side as they were, Sian had to admit reluctantly that Joshua was another man who paled next to Matt's settled, virile maturity.

'But you know what they say about youth being wasted on the young,' remarked Matt with pointed silkiness, as his fierce hazel eyes met and locked with his brother's.

Sian bit her lip as Joshua bridled visibly and snapped back, 'Just because you're young doesn't mean you can't know your own mind!'

'No, but it does mean that you have a great deal of inexperience in knowing what to do when you change your mind,' replied Matt coolly, his voice at complete odds with the anger that sparked like black lightning from the depths of his darkening gaze.

Sian looked yearningly across the laughing people who were enjoying themselves, oblivious to the storm gathering in their midst. She turned her attention back to the men who were glaring at each other over her head. Over her head! This bone most certainly did not agree to the contention, and said in a dangerously soft voice, 'Let's clear the air, shall we?'

Joshua recalled himself with a start. Matt merely raised his eyebrows, and his weary, sardonic expression was the final straw that broke her sorely tried patience and ignited her fuse. Sian's eyes blazed and she bit out succinctly, 'Your brother, Joshua, has seen fit to tell me that he does not approve of our engagement! I, on the other hand, had to hear myself denounced at unflattering length in my own home by a total stranger. Now, you two can fight among yourselves all you like, and it is no concern of mine! However, you will not do so at my birthday party, in my time!'

Joshua fell back a step in astonishment, for Matt had been right earlier; he had never seen her lose her temper before but she was far too gone in her butane heat to care.

Well into her stride, she rounded on Matt in fine fury, strands of her hair flicking along ivory collarbones like ribbons of black silk. 'And you! I have never met a more rude, arrogant, overbearing and blindly prejudiced man in my life! You ought to be ashamed of yourself, though I suspect in saying so I am merely wasting my breath! If Joshua, or any other man, does me the honour of proposing marriage, I will accept or reject him strictly on the merits of our relationship, and believe me, you have a snowball's chance in hell of being able to influence my decision one way or the other! I have *not* enjoyed your company, you may leave at your soonest convenience, goodnight!'

Oh, the awful nerve of the man; Matt grinned, swift and slightly incredulous, shedding his former demeanour of ennui. He looked so satirically entertained that Sian's temperature shot sky-high. Her vision dimmed and blurred, and, in one beautifully controlled expression of purest rage, she dumped her laden plate together with the wine down the front of his shirt.

Someone gasped in the dead silence. Sian suspected that it might have come from her. She stared up into the sudden, deadly calm of his face and it was like looking down the twin barrels of a shotgun. With supreme and enviable poise Matt brought up a hand, and she flashed back to the scene by the tree when she'd thought he was going to slap her.

His savage gaze held her prisoner. With one forefinger he hooked one dollop of creamy potato salad off his white shirt and brought it to his lips to suck it off.

Shock sizzled down the raw nerve-endings of her every limb at the sheer sensuality of the act, while the worldly hazel eyes mocked and challenged and baited. He smiled, smoky and satanic; she tossed her luxuriant head in disdain and all but stamped her foot. A slight gust of wind lifted her hair and blew it across her face in a transparent midnight veil, through which could be seen the lovely shape and colour of her unwinking eyes.

The moment of frozen tableau passed Jane was suddenly present, interposing her small body between Matt and Sian while babbling about accidents and washing machines and detergents. The world moved and breathed and lived again, but Matt and Sian still stared at each other with the naked aggression of two boxing opponents, insulated in their own electrical current.

This was war, and Sian no longer cared about the how or the why of it; she only knew that it sang a hot fusion to the juddering blood in her veins.

CHAPTER TWO

SIAN had a quick word with Jane and left the party at around two o'clock to spend the night at a girlfriend's apartment, frankly running from the overwhelming events of the day. Late the next morning, which was as bright and promised to be as hot as the day of the party, she showered and dressed quickly in a pale rose bikini, over which she wore a matching pink vest top and a blue miniskirt, showing a good length of the long slim, perfectly muscled legs that Jane yearned for.

Karen, a manager of a local restaurant that didn't close on Memorial Day, had already left for work. Sian wrote her a note of thanks for letting her sleep on the couch, then stuffed various toiletries into her hastily packed overnight bag.

She didn't care if her running away from the party had been transparent; she had badly needed time to herself. She had pleaded tiredness as an excuse to escape Matt's tenacious presence. Just thinking about Joshua's older brother brought her blood to a low simmer.

It had been no use telling herself that he'd had to hang around while his shirt tumbled through a wash, then the drying cycle. It had certainly been no use telling herself that she only had her own hot temper to blame. For whatever reason, he had been there, tall and tough and bare-chested, like a great wild tawny animal that had prowled into the house for a nap. Laughing at the things Jane had said. Talking quietly at some length to a fuming and subdued Joshua in one corner.

That she had hated to witness. Joshua had acted as if Matt were his father or something—rebellious, resentful and still with the challenging bravado of the male adolescent, yet reined and under control by his older brother's tough, authoritative presence.

Gone was the delightful young adult, the witty and articulate law student, and in his place sat a sheepish little boy. Sian had seen Joshua through Matt's eyes, and she hadn't appreciated the experience. Matt might feel responsible for his younger brother, but he was not Joshua's father and could not take the place of that man, who had died some years ago.

She quickly and efficiently put her hair back into a sleek french braid, then left her friend's apartment. Sian, Jane, Jane's boyfriend Steven, and Joshua were going to Lake Michigan for the day, and she was determined to enjoy the holiday as much as possible.

Chances were that, after her impassioned speech last night, Joshua would be scared off from proposing for good. His older brother would have gone back to Chicago some time this morning, and that would be that. The whole situation was simple, really, just a storm in a teacup in the cosmic scope of things, and Sian could get back to her uncomplicated life. By the time she had driven back to her own place, she had firmly resolved to put the annoying Matt Severn out of her mind.

The original plan had been that everybody would help clean up, then take off to the Indiana Dunes in two cars. But when Sian went through the back gate, the garden was already clean and tidy. She looked around in surprise. All the signs of the party were cleared away and several full black plastic bags were piled neatly by the kitchen door.

The apartment was similarly neat and, after last night, echoed with emptiness. The muted sound of the shower came from the direction of the bathroom. Shaking her head in bemusement, for Jane had never before shown such initiative for housekeeping, Sian travelled down the hall and put a hand on the doorknob of her bedroom.

The door opened inwards, and it was not propelled by her. Caught off balance and still in motion, she collided with a very large body. Two hands shot out to grip her arms; her own, outstretched, splayed flat on a lean bare torso. For one sulphurous moment she felt surprisingly silken skin, the sinuous rippling of hard abdominal muscle, and she snatched her hand back as if she'd been burned while staring wide-eyed up into Matt Severn's tough, formidable face.

She gasped, as her world tilted, 'You!'

'Me!' agreed Nick mockingly, his hazel gaze snapping with some volcanic emotion.

His hands were large and warm, and curled easily around the circumference of her upper arms. He shifted them down to her elbows, and the sensation of those callused palms sliding along her sensitive skin was so shockingly intimate that she recoiled violently. 'What are you doing here in my room?' she demanded, feeling exposed and invaded.

'Making the bed,' he said. Then, at her furious glare, he added with a careless shrug, 'I had to sleep somewhere, didn't I?'

Sian looked around a broad, tanned shoulder at the neat peach-coloured bedspread. It looked just as she had left it the day before, but a mental image of his long male body stretched out between her sheets, his rather long tawny hair spilling on to the pillow, produced the strangest reaction in the pit of her stomach. Swallowing hard and frowning fiercely, she muttered, 'Why didn't you just go home?'

'Temper,' he chided, then moved with silent, menacing deliberation to shut the door behind her. When she made an involuntary, protesting movement, he turned to lean against the panels, blocking the exit. 'I was over the drinking limit. You wouldn't have wanted me to cause a car accident, would you?'

'No, of course not!' she snapped, throwing her bag down on the floor in an impetuous gesture, inwardly struggling against a deep sense of unease at how he had trapped her into this confrontation.

His searing gaze was like two gold coins; he was as angry as he had ever been with her yesterday, Sian saw, and she was bewildered, for surely the break from hostilities should have cooled things down. 'Where did you sleep, darling, and with whom?' he queried silkenly.

Match to dry tinder. Sian was bravely aware of what she did, as she bent with striking speed to snatch up her overnight case and hurl it at his head. He hardly moved. One powerful arm flexed, and the case was caught in mid-air.

His expression was frightening. She snarled, 'Get away from that door!'

'As you wish.' He pushed off from the barrier behind him, and began to stalk towards her, his half-clad body overwhelmingly powerful, those deep disturbing eyes of his afire.

She folded her arms tight across her chest, cupping her elbows, and fought an instinctive desire to back away from him skittishly. She would not let him intimidate her, especially here on her own home territory. It was where people psychologically felt most secure and relaxed; that was why they felt so violated when their homes were broken into. Not only were personal possessions lost forever, but their security was stolen as well. She suspected that his choice of venue for a private confrontation was made knowing fully well what kind of advantages he might hope to gain.

But Sian had moved around so much when she was young that she had instinctive guards erected against that sort of thing. Home and security were not the walls that surrounded her; home was where the heart was, and she carried hers with her. People mattered, not places or things, and, though this had been her bedroom for the last four years, in the end it was just another room. Sian had her poise back, and her angry, delicate face was thrown back as she faced him with an unflinching, unrepentant glare. She could have hurt him with the heavy case. She didn't care.

Matt murmured speculatively, his attention focused on her like a spearthrust, 'You weren't with Joshua—you left far too early for that.'

She sneered at him, 'How do you know we didn't meet later?'

'You ran away from me, didn't you? Coward,' he accused her mockingly, bringing a hand up to the taut lines of her jaw.

She jerked her face away and spat, 'Don't touch me! My God, you've got an inflated sense of yourself, and my sleeping arrangements are none of your damned business! Why don't you go back to where you came from?'

'But, darling,' he purred from low in his chest, his naked golden chest that was making her crazy, 'I'm on vacation as well. That's why, when Joshua told me he intended to marry you, I decided to come and see how things were for myself.'

'Well,' she drawled, lips curling sardonically while her stomach turned into a hard rock of nerves, 'we all know how successful *that* turned out to be. And what did Joshua think about all this?'

'He thought it was a good idea, actually,' was Matthew's surprising reply, albeit said in an extremely dry tone of voice. His eyes were all over her. She felt as if she were being eaten alive. 'Obviously one look at you was supposed to dispel all my preconceived notions.'

Sian's jaw flexed against a furtive, psychic bruise and the expression in her own gaze went flat and dead. The implication that even in person she did not meet up to his high standards was insultingly obvious, and she absolutely hated her own inability to prevent this man from so casually hurting her. She said, choked, 'I've had enough of this abuse.'

'I haven't finished yet.'

He held her, two hands on her slim shoulders, with damnable ease. There was a high flush under her creamy skin, a tight line to her normally soft mouth, an unconscious shift to defensiveness in her posture.

Matt frowned. He said clearly and forcefully, 'Listen to me. For some time Joshua has been coming home full of admiring stories in which a certain Sian Riley figured largely. He talked about Sian's poise and wit, and the clever way she could manoeuvre a situation to gain the advantage. Sian had travelled all over the world, and had famous rock-star friends and midnight swims off private yachts in the Mediterranean. Sian was the life and soul of the party. Sian told him just exactly how to manipulate a difficult professor. Sian cleaned out all his friends in a poker game, so that he had to ask for an advance on his next month's allowance.'

Her eyes grew gradually larger and more bewildered as he spoke, for the person he was talking about wasn't her. Everything he said had an element of truth to it, but the emphasis was all wrong.

Was that really how Joshua saw her? What about all the characteristics *she* considered important, like her sense of humour, compassion, and caring? The picture Matt was portraying was a figure made of cake icing, all soft and frothy and without real substance. When at the last he mentioned the poker game, she could no longer remain silent.

'That stupid game!' she cried angrily, moving under his grip with sharp impatience. 'I didn't even want to play but they were so insistent, so determined to pit their wits against someone who had been taught by a legend— my father! You don't know what it was like.'

'I have been to university myself, once upon a time,' he reminded her drily. 'I know what kind of idiotic macho stunts get pulled. So you took all their money from them.'

'What was I supposed to *do*—give it back?' she retorted. 'That might have been convenient for *you*, but their pride would never have allowed it! It was better they were taught a lesson by somebody who knew when to stop, instead of meeting up one day with a card shark who would get them into real trouble.'

'Such a hard woman,' he drawled, one corner of his mouth pulled in deep, scoring that dimpled crease into one lean cheek.

If only she was! If only she could find some way to unmake that deep-seated need of hers to be accepted and become entirely self-sufficient, so that people like Matthew could never find their way past her defences to wound her with careless words! A dark shadow of self-mockery crossed her face and she said bitterly, 'Is that how you see me?'

'I didn't say that I didn't agree with you, or that I wouldn't have done the same under the circumstances,' he pointed out impatiently. 'I'm merely explaining how you come across, from what Joshua was telling me. *That's* the person I was warning away yesterday, don't you understand? Whereas in reality you turned out to be something—quite different.'

She didn't understand the strange note in his voice. All she could grasp was that his explanation was nearly an apology. She was staggered, and, to cover up her reaction, said quickly, 'Ouch! Admitting that must have hurt. And how did Joshua take it, when you told him?'

Matt raised a single, haughty eyebrow and laughed so softly that Sian's colour rose again as she realised what she had betrayed by her question. If he'd had suspicions before about her implication that she'd spent the night with Joshua, now he knew for sure.

His hands relaxed and caressed her shoulders. He told her with cutting deliberation, 'I didn't tell him anything. This was between you and me, and it wasn't any of his business. I did tell him that I still considered you completely unsuitable for him. He does not have my approval on any proposal of marriage; I'll do everything in my power to keep it from happening, and from here on in he's on his own.'

After everything else he had just said, that was like a slap in the face. Blank outrage had Sian's jaw dropping wide open, then it shut with a snap that jarred her teeth and she said violently, 'Damn you, Matt Severn, I'll tell you just what you can do with all your presumptuous meddling——'

He was inexplicable. All traces of his former anger had quite dissipated somewhere in the course of the conversation, and now he laughed aloud, his hazel eyes twin windows to devilry. It silenced her as nothing else could have. He took hold of her French braid and tugged at it. Her head fell back as she stared up at him, stunned and immobilised, as he brought his face down until they were nose to nose, eye to perplexed, molten eye.

'Joshua,' said Matt with a white, keen smile, 'took it like a man. On the other hand, you, I'm glad to say, are taking it just like a woman.'

My God! she thought gibberingly—it looked—it seemed—after all he'd said and done, he wasn't about to try to *kiss* her...?

Matt's gaze lowered to the exposed line of her vulnerable throat, then lowered further to roam along the lines of her vest top. He stopped suddenly, masculine body frozen and breathing arrested, and the oddest expression flickered across the hard lines of his face.

She watched him in frozen confusion, and unable to protest anything. He bent, not to her lips, but to her arm. Surprise and a deep searing of lightning sensation trembled through her. Her upper arm, slim, the fragile creamy skin so prone to easy bruising, showed the clear imprint of his hold on her from the day before.

Matthew's mouth stroked the marks, nibbling at her flesh, the hand that was so offensive at the party now cupping the curve of her elbow as gently as if it were an eggshell.

Her breathing was ragged, severely disrupted. Her jaw clenched. Her mouth worked. Her head bowed over his angled shoulder; she could not tear her eyes away from the incredible sight of him. She did not know if she looked at him in tenderness, or in fury.

Just when she had wrested enough control from her shuddering mind and body to blast him clear to California, he let go of her with his face set and rigid, straightened, turned on his heel and left. The door settled gently into place again, and she was alone.

Sian's hands crept to her heated face. She was burning up all over from anger and excitement; she felt as if she were spinning like a top. She tried to encompass the enormity of what had just happened, but her turbulent, seething emotions were just too powerful to grapple with and all her usual poise had flown clean out of the window so long ago that it couldn't be recalled in a hurry.

That—that man. There wasn't anything awful enough, wide enough, deep enough to describe how confounding, fluctuating, provoking, exasperating he was. He left her floundering and stole away all her sense of proportion. Once she had considered herself experienced, but Matt was a mushroom cloud surpassing anything she could ever have imagined.

Of just one thing she was certain. He had an innate talent for making her angrier than she'd ever been before! Sian picked her bag up from the floor and surrendered to the same insane impulse that had made her chuck it to begin with. It smashed into the wall above the bed where he had slept, then slid into a satisfyingly humble heap on to the floor.

Well. That felt good. But it wasn't good enough.

Twenty minutes later, Sian came out of her bedroom with the canvas bag in which she had packed her sun lotion, dark glasses, a clean towel, comb and a small plastic pack filled with cleansing tissues.

Steven and Jane rode in Matt's Mercedes sports coupé while Sian rode with Joshua, glad for the opportunity to have a long overdue talk with him.

The sky was cloudless and it was steaming hot. Sian put on her sunglasses and climbed into Joshua's car, and was quiet and thoughtful during the first part of the forty-five-minute drive up to Lake Michigan, very conscious of the sleek, purring red sports car that shadowed Joshua's sedan.

Finally Joshua said, with a sideways glance and a tentative smile, 'Mad at me?'

'At you!' she exclaimed with a little laugh as she turned to him. 'Why should I be mad at you?'

His expression eased somewhat, but he still looked anxious and uncertain. 'For not having the courage to just come right out and ask you to marry me. For going to my brother instead. Sian, you have to understand. Matt's always been there for me. He's more like an uncle than an older brother—so capable and assured and interested in what I'm doing. I honestly didn't expect him to react the way he did.'

His eyes pleaded with her, and she stifled an impatient urge to grab him by the shoulders and shake him. He looked so earnest and handsome, tall and clean-limbed and graceful, but she just couldn't see him in quite the same way as she had before the party, or that talk with Matt in her bedroom.

Joshua was a beautiful golden boy. He admired the superficial aspects of her life and had made her into some kind of plastic idol. How dashing and exciting she must seem to him, with her exotic experiences and cosmopolitan outlook on life! No wonder he was infatuated, but where was the depth of perception and width of understanding in that? Where was the meeting of equals, the consent of kindred minds that saw and desired mutual goals in life?

She realised, then, that the kind of lasting relationship she wanted was one that had to be built on maturity and steadfastness that would produce the kind of stable, nurturing environment in which children could be raised. Joshua couldn't provide that for her, and it would be unfair to both of them to ever try to pretend otherwise. If she married him, she would be a mother but never a wife.

'I do love you,' he said softly, and she sighed. There was that four-letter word again, complicating things, scrambling the brains of otherwise intelligent people and turning life into a comedy of manners. Why couldn't everyone see what a mess it made of things, and that everything was so much more simple if one stuck to the gentle emotions like affection and respect?

'I love you too, darling,' she told him and gently touched his arm. 'But I don't think it means the same thing to me as it does to you.'

His face fell. Oh, dear, he looked as if he'd just been denied a particularly succulent ice-cream cone. She really must find some way to stop comparing him to a child! He muttered, 'Does that mean that there isn't any hope?'

'I think probably yes, it does,' she said quietly. 'I don't know how things will work out in the future, but right now it doesn't look very realistic. We've gone out together and had a good time, and we enjoy each other's company, but that isn't enough to support the kind of lifelong relationship you're proposing, is it?'

He looked out of his open window, brooding and unhappy but not, she noticed wryly, heartbroken. She just sat back and waited, and, after a few minutes, he stirred himself to say grimly, 'So Matt was right after all.'

Her sharp indrawn breath whistled in her throat. Underneath all the personality conflicts was an essential core of truth, and she replied with stiff honesty, 'Much as it pains me to say so, yes. But, Joshua—that doesn't mean he has to know it, does it?'

His head snapped around and he stared at her, before jerking his attention back to the road, and a slow smile of pure enjoyment broke the unhappiness that had darkened his youthful face. 'You really have it in for him, don't you?'

'I'm no peacemaker,' she admitted, green eyes snapping. 'And he did start it.'

'Talk about the warring Irish!' he chortled with joyous mischievousness. 'Matt does tend to have a rather provoking smugness whenever he's in the right. I'd say he deserves to be knocked down a peg or two, just once in his life. So what do you say—let's get engaged for a while to rub his nose in it.'

Sian brooded out of her window, black brows slanted. He'd be absolutely livid when he found out. What perfect, sublime revenge for the way he'd treated her! 'All right,' she grinned back recklessly. 'You're on. But let me be the one to tell him. I want to wait for just the right moment to drop the bombshell.'

Joshua frowned. 'Are you sure you know what you're doing? Matt can be very forceful when he's roused.'

'Don't worry about that. I can handle him.'

Why, Sian Riley, said her father's lyrical voice at the back of her head, 'tis a bigger liar you are than even I am. But she squelched the ghost firmly, because whether she could handle Matt or not, she was bound and determined to get him, just once and good. Regardless of the consequences. Like Joshua said, he certainly deserved it and she—she had a whole lot of bent pride that demanded payment.

Joshua pulled on to a side street and they cut through a quiet neighbourhood until they reached the house of a friend of his where they could leave the cars. The beach was about half a mile's walk along a forest path that followed a stream through several wide picnic clearings. As they climbed out and retrieved their bags from the car, the red Mercedes slid up behind them.

Jane and Steven had glowing eyes and high colouring and looked as though they had enjoyed themselves immensely. Matt wore an indulgent smile, layered tawny hair whipped off his forehead. He hadn't troubled to put on a shirt and the longest bottom strands lay along the golden tanned skin at the base of his neck. Sian's eyes moved all over him, from the amusement in his face to the expanse of his broad muscled chest. She couldn't help herself.

He glanced at her, caught her looking at him and his lazy grin widened. She stiffened before she could control it, then a deliberate reminder of the mischief she had in store for him brought a remarkably sweet smile to her lips. That took him aback, she saw with deep satisfaction, and a wary look crept into those clever hazel eyes. Her mood turned sunny.

The men carried the heavy coolers of food and drink while Jane and Sian carried the bags, and after walking through the forest for several minutes they came upon the dunes. The heat rising off the sand brought a light sheen of sweat to Sian's face, and she mopped her brow as she trudged behind Matt and Joshua. The closer they came to the blue sparkling lake that seemed as immense to the eye as any ocean, the more people they found.

'Whew!' said Jane, coming up beside her. The men had stopped and were discussing the best place to settle. 'Everybody and their uncle must be here.'

'And their brother,' added Sian in a dry undertone, at which the other girl giggled.

Joshua was asking, of nobody in particular, 'Should we try to get closer to the water?'

Matt said, one long, elegant hand shading his eyes, 'Why don't we try for slightly higher ground? The sun's quite strong and we ought to try to spread the blankets close to some shade if we can.'

He had sent a quick glance down Sian's body as he spoke, and, though he hadn't specifically said so, she knew that he had made the suggestion in deference to her pale creamy skin. The thoughtfulness surprised her.

At last they chose a site on a rise about thirty feet up from the beach by the water, the blankets spread half in the sunlight, half in the shade of a nearby copse that also worked as an effective windscreen. Then everybody settled into the business of some serious relaxation.

Jane rummaged in her large tote bag until she produced a black and white soccer ball, which she bounced off Steven's head when his back was turned. With a startled roar he leapt to his feet and she ran off laughing.

Sian smiled as she watched their carefree antics. There were no haggard signs of the stress they had all gone through in the last month as they struggled to finish papers and study for final exams. She and Jane had stalked around the apartment, short-tempered through lack of sleep and snapping at each other over the most ridiculous things.

Still, the work had been worth it. Sian was well qualified to seek out a position as a junior designer in a fashion house, though that wasn't what she wanted to do. She nursed a secret ambition to set up her own design company but lacked the self-confidence in how to go about doing it in such a cut-throat industry. It was why she had decided to continue going to school so that she could supplement her knowledge of design with courses in marketing and business administration. That way she stood a better chance of at least some modest success. She wasn't looking to make her fortune. She just wanted to earn a good living with some degree of independence.

Lost in contemplation of the future, she began to strip off her clothes absent-mindedly, completely unaware of the sudden still attention she attracted. Off came the pink top, revealing the pale rose bikini that moulded like a second skin over high rounded breasts. Down slid the elastic band of the skirt over a long, narrow waist, widening to a soft rounded belly and shapely hips. Her flawless ivory skin was so thin that delicate blue shadows could be seen in the strong sunlight at temples and wrists, the bottom of her soft beating throat, the backs of her knees.

She had just reached down for her bottle of water-resistant sun lotion when two long, athletically muscled legs entered her peripheral vision. Matt murmured silkily into her ear, stirring the tiny sensitive hairs at the nape of her neck, 'Like me to rub some of that on to your back?'

Joshua had appropriated the ball, and Jane and Steven chased him down into the water, the trio laughing maniacally. Sian turned to look at Matt with a wide gaze more green than long whipped strands of sea oats and grasses. She smiled at him pleasantly. 'Yes, thank you.'

Startlement flickered past the mischief in his own hazel eyes. Got him again, she thought with satisfaction, but he recovered himself with admirable ease and took the bottle to squeeze a portion into one large hand. She put her back to him and pulled her braid to one side while he started to rub her shoulders.

She had steeled herself for the alien sensation of his touch roaming by consent over her body, but found she was relaxing almost immediately under the warm surprise of his extremely gentle hands. He worked over the muscles of her back with unhurried sensitivity, discovering knots of tension and kneading them loose with care. Her head began to droop as she gave an unconscious sigh of pleasure.

'What happened to the open warfare?' he asked. The smile had carried to his voice.

She said, 'It's gone underground in a change of tactics. I believe they call it "low-intensity conflict".'

She felt rather than heard his laugh. Low and husky, it reverberated through his hands to her body, and her heart missed a beat. 'You won't give up, will you?'

'Is the Pope Catholic?' she returned sweetly. 'Besides, you don't strike me as the kind of person who would give up easily yourself.'

'You're right. I don't, especially when I see something I want. Then I go after it, and nothing short of flood, fire or act of God can make me stop,' he murmured.

She could well understand that. He wouldn't have got where he was today as a valued and respected senior partner for a huge multinational architectural firm if he hadn't had that unswerving drive to mould his actions. Certainly she had caught the backlash of his aggression; unleashed and in full force at the workplace, it would be something to see. His was the kind that erected towers and moved mountains.

'I stand warned,' she said, and hoped the quiver of her voice could be attributed to an answering amusement, instead of the real cause which was the unbelievable magic he was working on her body.

He reached up to massage the exposed nape of her neck and she must have made some sound, for the pressure in his fingers immediately eased and he asked, 'Did I hurt you?'

'No,' she replied, muffled. 'My neck's just stiff because I slept on it wrong.'

Then she almost flinched, half expecting another sardonic remark about her sleeping habits. Instead Matt said gently, 'Where, over here? Hold still a minute. There, how does that feel?'

Sian turned her head experimentally and said, surprised, 'Much better, thank you.'

'You're welcome,' he told her, then purred, 'Want me to do your front?'

She threw back her head and laughed out loud, the sound like music in the air, and held out her hand for the lotion. 'Not on your life! The warfare hasn't gone *that* far underground!'

He shifted to settle on the sand beside her, looping his arms around upraised knees, showing no inclination to join the others who were cavorting in the water. She shifted her gaze away from the flex of those powerful-looking biceps and bent her attention to applying lotion to the rest of her body.

After they had sat watching the swimmers and the silence had stretched to several minutes into something like peace, Matt turned his head and looked at her. 'It won't work, you know.'

'What won't?' she asked, startled and wary.

'What you're trying to do.' He regarded her with a cool, measuring stare and said, soft and deliberate, 'I'm no young, inexperienced boy you can get around by using your charm.'

The predator was back, curled and waiting his moment in the sun for a chance to spring, the hard eyes unblinking on her sun-flushed face, that mobile mouth taut. But for the first time Sian saw past the impact his forcefulness had on her and smiled. It was nice to see him doing the reacting for a change.

An attempt at innocence would be a mistake, for he had been right. She leaned back on her elbows and returned stare for stare. 'Is that what you think I'm trying to do?'

'I think,' he said slowly, not returning her smile, 'that you would try to charm the leaves off the trees if you thought it would be to your advantage.'

Sian's eyes narrowed, a quick, telling gesture; and the slim lines of her eyebrows became tokens of unpredictability. She said abruptly, 'People are like circles, don't you think?'

His face became shuttered, the thoughts moving behind the mask with subterranean speed. After a moment he asked, 'How so?'

She drew him a picture in the sand, slim forefinger moving lightly through the grains, of circles interlocking. 'Like so. Joshua sees this part of my circle, and he thinks what he sees is me. Part of it is, but that isn't all I am. We show different aspects of our personalities to different people; we assume roles. Child to parent, friend to friend, lover to lover, enemy to enemy.'

The quick hazel eyes lifted lightly to her face, the sun reflecting out of his eyes in vivid sparks. 'And which are you?' he asked. Probing, ever probing. 'Child, friend, lover, or enemy?'

The lines of her face were pared, stripped of every social convention, clean of animation until what was left was a patient and unforgiving intelligence.

'You drew a circle of all those preconceived notions about who I am, and what I would do,' she said quietly, and clenched her fist in the sand of her drawing. The tendons stood out, dusted with gold. 'You think you've dropped your original ones, but you've only gone on to form others. You're just so arrogant, Matt. That's your biggest failing and that's how I'm going to get you, because, every time you turn your back on me, I'll be jumping out of the circle.'

CHAPTER THREE

MATT just continued to watch her, large and powerful as some transcendant classic, enigmatic as the Sphinx. In the glare of the unrelenting sun his brown face showed marks of imperfection that made his handsomeness so very human. There was a dangerous attraction in the tiny laugh-lines fanning from his eyes and the faint signs of exhaustion that lingered from recent overwork, for they made him all that more approachable. He was no invincible juggernaut; he was a man, with more than his fair share of a man's strengths and not a few of the failings.

With an inward shiver, she steeled herself against such observations, for she could not afford to soften. One slide into the tender side of her emotions and she would be in trouble. In that one respect he was like her father, for he too was a soul-stealer, one of that rare breed that women invariably fell for all over the world. He could lay his tawny head against a woman's breast and call forth all the feelings Sian was so determined to avoid, accept them as his due, and then walk away without a backward glance. He was more than dangerous; he was lethal.

'You're not a forgiver, are you, Sian?' he commented, almost absently. The keen focus of his attention took apart the definition of her.

'No, I'm not much of a forgiver,' she agreed, after a moment of deadly silence. It was an acknowledgement made in honesty, without pride or prevarication. Fair warning, tit for tat. An eye for an eye.

Then, quietly, he said an astonishing thing. 'I hadn't realised that I had hurt you so much.'

Reaction animated her expression as her green eyes flared, and she turned her head away in a harsh jerk that sent her french braid whipping over one shoulder. 'Did you?' she returned, with the faintest mocking edge of vicious rejoinder. 'Or did you just get in my way?'

'Are you so sure,' asked Matt then, wise and gentle as he bent forward over her half-reclining body, 'that I'm the one with the preconceived notions now, and not you?'

The change in his position cast a shadow over her face. She glanced up swiftly. He was a silhouette against the vast bright bowl of the sky, and all she could see was the outline of his head, which contained some fugitive quality that brought an unconscious parting of her dry lips. The tip of her pink tongue darted out to moisten them, and some slight change in the inclination of his head made her extremely aware of the act and shortened her breath.

He whispered, and the sound of it came over her like a warm breeze, 'All I said to you earlier was that I considered you unsuitable for Joshua, and you are. You're far too strong and volatile for someone as young and inexperienced as he, even down to the lovely curves and graceful shape of your perfect body. He hasn't got the capacity to give you the depth of emotion and quality of passionate lovemaking that you deserve. If you marry him, you will always ache for what you don't have, and he will always feel inadequate without quite understanding why.'

She trembled and longed to take the weight of her torso off the uncertain strength in her arms, but if she tried to sit up now she would bring herself within inches of his face, and the ravishing devastation pouring forth from that sexy, ruthless mouth. So, rather than moving towards him, she tried to attack instead. 'Maybe somebody like Joshua has just what I'm looking for,' she mocked, wishing her voice didn't sound so husky. 'After all, you can't control his money forever.'

Matt sounded amused. 'I had that one coming, didn't I? All right, Sian, I take it back unreservedly. A person who could handle that poker game the way you did, with reluctance, finesse and compassion, could never settle for a shallow, short-sighted goal such as money. What are you really looking for?'

The insight that she had only recently wished for in Joshua was present in abundance in his older brother, but Sian did not rejoice in the finding of it. Instead she felt exposed and self-protective.

'Try stability, for one,' she said, her tone clipped. 'Plenty of people build secure relationships on other things besides love and passion, which can fizzle out so easily once the honeymoon stage of the marriage is over.'

'Could you actually settle for a marriage of convenience?' He made the question into a statement of incredulity, twisting her meaning into a concept that sounded unacceptable. 'Would you really do something like that to a man like Joshua who was in love with you? If I were you, I would think about that long and hard, because it seems to me that there's an element of cruelty in it, especially if you were to fall in love with someone else.'

'No, of course I wouldn't!'

'Ah,' he stated flatly, 'then you would marry a man who wasn't in love with you.'

'Love doesn't have to come into it!' she replied heatedly, impatient scorn crossing her upturned expression. 'Everybody always makes so much of love and marriage going hand in hand, when stability and constancy are the important factors—and passionate affairs are distinctly overrated, when all they appear to bring are confusion and unhappiness to the parties concerned! Love is fine for those who want it, but it doesn't hold the least part in my plans, thank you very much! I prefer my heart just the way it is—whole and unbroken!'

'Now I begin to get a picture of your Utopia,' remarked Matt coolly. 'Polite conversation at the breakfast table and a weekly, joyless performance of your conjugal duties. Heaven help your children if you achieve your dream, because a more sterile existence I cannot imagine.'

She could no longer remain where she was and twisted sideways to rise out from under him. 'That's because you subscribe to the popular belief that one has to be in love to be happy,' she retorted over her shoulder, brushing away the grains of sand that clung to her elbows. 'Whereas I am happy just the way I am, and I fully intend on staying that way!'

'Unawakened, unfulfilled, untouched,' he murmured, a snake in the garden of paradise. 'Take care to build your briars very high, sleeping princess, otherwise real life will creep in when you least expect it.'

'Rubbish,' she said in a strong voice, but she crossed her arms defensively around a shaken stomach.

He continued, as if he hadn't heard her, 'And I'll tell you this for nothing. Yes I believe in love, because, unlike you, I have been in love before, and it was not the naïve, helpless emotion you seem to think it is but a full-blooded, enriching experience in which passion and serenity were equal partners.'

Sian's head turned. When he stopped, she asked, 'What happened?'

He said quietly, 'She died of cancer when she was twenty-five.'

'I'm sorry,' she said just as quietly, as she turned around fully to look at him with deep compassion. 'How terrible.'

He smiled at her. 'But somehow it wasn't. Her grace and spirit wouldn't allow it to be. She's gone, and has been for quite some time, but I will never forget her. Because of what she taught me, I can say categorically that I will never marry without that depth and immensity of feeling. My wife will be so totally and completely in love with me that she will give her heart gladly into my safekeeping, and I will guard it and nurture it as the most precious possession on earth. I'll have to, you see, for mine will be given to her. Completely, down to the last humble flaw, always and forever. That's what real love is, Sian, not infatuation, not mere sexuality, not the heat of the moment. Anything else by comparison is a poor substitute.'

She didn't question the impulse that made her lay a light hand on the warmth of his forearm, nor stint the sincere generosity of her reply. That was how far in he had reached. By laying down the tools of hardness and aggression, by baring his soul and revealing his own vulnerable, unquenchable hope, he had managed to win this round without a fight, and he won so well that she didn't even begrudge him the victory. 'It sounds a fine, rare thing. I hope you find it.'

He took her hand, raised it to his lips and kissed it. 'Oh, I will, never fear,' he said, then added with a sultry purr, 'The only trouble will be in convincing her that she wants it as badly as I do.'

Sian smiled and drew away. 'There's the crunch,' she said drily. 'Everybody's looking for something different out of life. You have your dreams and I have mine, and who's to say? Maybe we'll both get what we want.'

'But is Joshua really what you want, when it comes right down to it? Can his immature impression of who you are provide stability?' he asked, dissecting her with a shrewd level stare.

She hesitated, tempted to confess the real truth of what lay between her and his younger brother, for she no longer felt such a burning desire for revenge now that he had neatly taken the sting out of everything he'd said to her before.

The trouble with Matt was that he too was constantly shifting his tactics, with such subtle dexterity that she was forced to re-evaluate her position at every turn. The hunter in him was more dangerous than anything she had ever met, for he laid his snares with the seduction of gentleness, the insidious voice of logic and reason. If he was debilitating in head-on conflict, he was even more so in the oblique attack, for he hit his target with unfailing accuracy.

In the end she decided that silence was by far the wisest course, so she just smiled and said gently, 'That would be telling, wouldn't it?'

A sharp frown creased his forehead. He opened his mouth to say something, but their conversation was abruptly broken off as the soccer ball landed in his lap and Jane ran up to them. 'Come on, you two lazy-bones, quit sitting around and join the game!'

Matt rose with good grace, but Sian declined the rough-and-tumble sport, opting to go for a swim in-s..d. Floating in the silken warm water was deliciously refreshing after the heat-baked sand. She closed her eyes, drifting, thinking about everything Matt had said. Thinking of hopes, dreams, and forgiveness.

The rest of the day passed beautifully, with everyone settling into a quiet contentment. Voices gentled and bodies, well fed and bathed and kissed by the sun, reclined on picnic blankets. Even the raucous blare of radios from other distant camps couldn't break the serene spell. As the sun dipped towards the horizon, many of the other bathers began to leave; they would miss the best part of the day, Sian felt, for the wide sky remained cloudless and there would be a lovely sunset.

Her discussion with Matt had managed to clear the air as their earlier explosions had failed to do so. She was as relaxed as she had ever been, and had lost enough of her antipathy towards him to appreciate, as the others did, what good company he could be.

He had dropped any outward sign of his former antagonism, even cracking a joke or two, to which she laughed and the others, after the first frozen moment of uncertainty, laughed as well.

How clever he was. Sian studied him surreptitiously through her lashes. He could use his own charm with as much conscious effectiveness as she ever did, but she could not lay claim to the same impenetrability as he. A cold thrill shivered through her. Don't soften, Sian, she whispered to herself. Harden your heart.

Jane had turned somnolent and lay curled on her side, her head by Sian's thigh, drowsing as the others talked. Sian's fingers affectionately stroked the blonde hair away from her friend's temple as she listened, occasionally interposing a quiet comment. Matt glanced their way often with a smile; she could see the male appreciation glinting in his eyes at the pretty picture they made.

At length Jane stirred and shivered, for the wind had picked up and the heat was going out of the day. Sian had already donned her pink top and had taken care not to stay out too long in the sun, but Jane's skin felt over-warm when she laid cool fingers along the other girl's cheek.

'You need your jacket,' she said softly, when Jane's eyes opened. 'Did you remember to bring it?'

'Yes, but I left it in the back seat of Matt's car,' murmured the other girl with a wide yawn.

'Would you like for me to fetch it?' she asked.

'Mmn, I need to wake up anyway.' Jane sat and ran her fingers through her hair. 'Want to walk with me?'

'Sure,' she agreed readily and rose to her feet. Steven had just coaxed Joshua into another swim. Matt sat watching the two dark heads arrow through the silver sparkling reflections on the very deep blue water, and turned enquiringly as she knelt beside him. 'Could we borrow your car keys, please? Jane's feeling a bit chilled and needs her jacket.'

'Of course.' He twisted at the waist and reached for his faded denim shorts that lay folded nearby, digging into one pocket. Left unobserved, Sian let her gaze roam freely with admiration over his lithe, powerful body in the brief trunks. That dark brown of his tanned skin looked like furred velvet, encasing an artist's composition of grace and strength. A searing vision of his male body, enmeshed and subjugated and arcing in spear-thrusting passion, imploded in her with such force that she gasped in silent distress.

He was too quick. His attention fixed on her flushed face, the green eyes cloudy, the barely discernible tremor in the slim fingers that took the jingling keys he offered.

Dear heaven, what had she done? She couldn't look at him. His hand snaked over hers compulsively, and tightened until the keys dug into her palm. 'Sian.'

The husky voice was raw, urgent, an enquiry. Her terrified gaze lifted. His hazel eyes had ignited with such ferocity that he looked nearly blind. 'Let me go,' she breathed, the plea carrying an intolerable weight of sweeping importance.

'For now,' he said. His hard fingers opened until her trembling fist lay free in the large palm. She snatched away as he whispered, 'Run away, little girl. For now.'

The sexuality inherent in that reply, coming like a bolt from the blue, crackled high-voltage tension all over her body. She fled back to Jane and scooped up her mini-skirt along the way, her composure in tatters. Her friend, fully alert now, gave her a very curious look but thankfully refrained from comment, and after five minutes of brisk walking Sian's temperature returned to normal.

They found the path through the forest easily enough, but, as the shallow stream offered a much more refreshing walk and a chance to rinse the sand from their feet, they decided to wade in it instead.

About halfway back to the cars, they came upon a group of four children who were dancing about in the water, in quite an agitated state. As soon as the largest, a girl of about eleven years old, saw them, she came splashing up and cried, 'Oh, please, please help us! My brother's climbed up the tree and he can't get down again! I told him not to do it, but he wouldn't listen to me! I'm afraid he's going to fall!'

The poor child was sobbing so hard she could barely talk, and Jane groaned; she had such a phobia for heights that even mention of them was enough to make her queasy. After her initial surprise, Sian said to the frightened girl with deliberate composure, 'Calm down, darling. It's all right. As long as he doesn't lose his grip or his head, he's not going to fall. Why don't you show us where he is, and then we'll see what we can do about getting him down, OK?'

The girl nodded, then turned and ran back the way she'd come, throwing great splashes of water that soaked Sian's legs as she followed. She didn't need the girl's upturned face and pointed finger, for, as soon as they approached the other children, her eyes were drawn up to the sound of high-pitched sobbing—up and up and up, to the very top of the great, twisted tree where the sun still shone on a bright patch of clothing.

Sian's breath whistled in horror and her heart thumped hard, for the boy's T-shirt was caught at the back on a jagged branch that must have broken underneath his weight, at about the height of a three-storey building, right where the branches were thin and willowy-young. Jane clutched her arm in an icy grip, for as they watched a gust of breeze blew through the tree and he swayed sickeningly from side to side, shrieking in terror.

'Oh, God, Sian, I—I think I'm going to be sick!'

Sian's initial shock faded in a wave of adrenalin. She rounded on her friend and snapped coldly, 'Stop that! You're frightening the other children.'

She had never used that tone of voice with Jane before, not even in her worst temper, and the other girl stiffened, shocked out of her internal reaction. 'Listen to me,' Sian said, her gaze hard and clear on the blonde's face. 'It's obvious he can't climb down by himself and, the way the poor brat's got himself twisted, he's going to fall if he doesn't stop panicking.'

'Call the fire department!' cried one of the children

'Even if you could find a phone, it wouldn't do any good,' Sian said. Her own face was rigid with enforced calm. 'They can't get their equipment this far back into the woods Someone's got to bring him down Where are your parents?'

The first girl who had hailed them said, wiping her tear-stained face, 'Back at the picnic site, that way.'

She pointed in the direction Sian and Jane had been heading. Sian nodded and said grimly, 'Go tell them what's happened. Now.'

She did not shout; she wouldn't have anyway, not in their state, but all four bolted as if they were fleeing from the wrath of God, and, at the sight of his friends disappearing, the boy at the top of the tree sobbed even harder.

'Hey!' Sian shouted, forcing a no-nonsense tone into her voice. 'Why's a big lad like you crying like that! You think that's high? I used to climb twice as high as that when I was half your size! Now, quit your snivelling and keep a firm grip, and we'll have you down before you know it!'

Jane was a shaken mess beside her, but at least she wasn't having hysterics. Sian said to her in a quiet undertone, 'The branches are too thin where he's stuck. Do you understand? Only someone small and light can climb that high. But it's obvious you can't do it, so there's only me. I'm going to try to get his shirt unstuck, but I don't think he can climb down on his own—he's far too frightened, and I'm not strong enough to carry him. Janey, we need help.'

Jane's eyes clung to her as she talked, and she was thankful to see that some rationality had crept into the other girl's huge eyes. 'Oh, Sian, be careful, for God's sake! If the branches are breaking under *his* weight——'

'Don't fall to pieces on me now!' snapped Sian. 'Just get help—and hurry!'

Jane stole one last look, shuddered and ran. Sian, too, turned to stare up at what had suddenly become an immeasurable, impossible distance and wished she could think of some other alternative. But there wasn't any and she knew it, so, before she lost her nerve, she gritted her teeth and started to climb.

The first half was easy; she could see how seductive the prank would be to the mind of a mischievous boy, and how foolishly he had let his self-confidence convince him that he could go higher than he should have. As soon as he sensed that help was on its way, he began to cry again in a mixture that she suspected was part renewed fear and part relief.

'What's your name?' she asked, selecting her next oranch with cold logical care and taking another step up. Her wet bare feet were drying quickly and finding purchase on the rough bark, though she knew she would have bruises afterwards on the soft skin of her inner sole.

There was a break in the outburst, then he said with a gulp, 'Barry.'

'Well, Barry, my name's Sian. S-i-a-n. That's Welsh for Jane, which is my friend's name as well. My mother came from Wales—it's a place, you know, not a big fish,' she told him conversationally, then paused. Sure enough, he had forgotten enough of his panic to produce a rather hollow chuckle, and she smiled wryly and continued, 'I know a story about a Welshman who thought he could fly. Would you like to hear it?'

'O-OK, sure.'

And so she began, and, as she talked to keep him calm and her mind off the very real danger of what she was doing, she was already reaching up for another branch.

CHAPTER FOUR

Sian had a vivid memory of when she was a very small child, not quite two years old, in which her mother, still living then, was a large shadowy figure. Her parents were already separated at that time, and once when Devin had come to visit his daughter she had run to him with arms outstretched.

He had swung her up into his strong arms, her big handsome father, and the world had reeled giddily about her as she chortled with delight. Then he had tossed her into the air and her bright uncontainable joy had immediately turned to fright as everything solid and secure had fallen away and she was left for one immeasurable instant suspended in mid-air.

The moment had passed too quickly for her to even cry out. Gravity had claimed her tiny body, and she fell, and her father caught her close into a great hug, and everything settled again into how it should be. But Sian had never forgotten that pure terror as she began to tumble helplessly back to the ground.

She had a mental flashback of it that broke her into a cold sweat as she rested, panting, for a few seconds and surveyed her position. Time had slowed and there was nothing but the present, and the quiet sound of leaves rustling. She had discovered another hazard in her climb, which was the slippery sun lotion that coated her body and made her confidence of her grip very shaky. Her arms were beginning to ache from the tight clench she maintained, but no hint of her fear filtered into her calm, even voice as she talked to the boy and listened for his occasional high treble of a reply.

She had reached the thinner branches and picked her way with extreme care, testing their strength before trusting her weight to them, and at each creak and sway her breath stopped in her throat and she froze before continuing to inch upwards.

It could not have been more than five minutes before the quiet surrounding the two in the tree was broken by the noisy approach of people. Sian risked a glance down. She could see in the group hurrying from the picnic site the same reactions that she and Jane had had, the shock of hesitation as they took in the scene, and the various positions of fright. Oh, lord, she thought in resignation, not a fit and athletic man among the lot of them.

A woman cried out in a high voice, and Barry started to sob again, quietly.

'Is that your mom? Not to worry,' said Sian, tilting back her head. She was at a level with one dirty sneaker, and it seemed very small and vulnerable as it dangled in front of her eyes. 'I bet she has a fit if you cross the street, doesn't she?'

'She's gonna kill me!' the boy burst out. Sian had room inside her for one breathless chuckle.

Preoccupied with soothing the child, trying to ignore the panic below her, Sian was unaware of another's approach to the scene. The man sprinted full out, with powerful distance-eating strides as swift at the end of the half-mile as when he'd begun, a gold and tawny figure spearing through the shallow water which cascaded from the force of his urgent passage into sparkling diamonds.

His intent expression did not change when he saw the trapped boy and Sian's slim body underneath, taut with striving feline grace, seemingly suspended at the top of the tree by insubstantial green fronds and a prayer. But his hazel eyes undertook a sharp dilation, and his chest moved hard, where before the headlong dash had barely quickened his heartbeat.

Then Sian heard the sound of another voice from the ground, deep and firm and commanding, and her knees went to water in an intense flood of relief as she recognised Matt taking charge of the threatening pandemonium. He had been amazingly fast; Jane had to have raced back to the camp as if all the hounds of hell were snapping at her heels.

He must have summed up the situation at a glance, for, without any of the horrified hesitation that had frozen the others, he called quietly, 'I'm coming up, Sian. Don't try to free him until I'm underneath you.'

'OK,' she said, and breathlessly waited as he swarmed up the tree with athletic ease. She risked a peek over her shoulder. He had stopped when the branches started to groan protestingly under his greater weight, and his serious upturned face was about ten feet below her.

Their eyes met: fatalistic, almond-shaped green and fierce hazel. Ten feet might as well have been an eternity. His expression was terrible and she closed her eyes to it. Sian heard the creak of another branch.

'Don't come any further.' Her tone was bloodless with terror. Another creaking, and Sian shuddered as if she'd been axed. 'For God's sake, Matthew!'

'Never mind about me,' Matt said with ruthless calm. 'Be very careful now. Can you hook your legs around the next branch and reach high enough to free him?'

'I can try.' She eased forward with infinite caution, her tired muscles aching in protest, and swallowed hard against vertigo as the wind sent the overburdened treetop swaying in an exaggerated arc. Then, after wrapping her legs tight around the fearfully slim trunk, she ran questing fingers up the boy's small back, straining upwards as far as she could. As soon as she had a firm grip on his T-shirt, she said gently, 'Right, Barry. I'm going to pull you loose. I want you to hold on as tight as you can. Don't panic if you feel a tug, because I've got you. Understand?'

'Y-yes.'

She gritted her teeth and tugged, and the T-shirt tore off the jagged edge it had been caught on. The boy screamed as he heard the material rip and he twisted like an eel to clutch, not at the trunk as she'd told him to, but at her hand.

She could feel it coming the split second before it happened. With the violent shift of his body, the boy lost his perch. She had no time to do more than to snake her hand around his wrist in a death clench before he went tumbling past her.

Then Sian screamed as well, as her torso was yanked backwards and both the boy and her back and shoulders slammed with stunning force against the trunk.

She hit her head and nearly blacked out. For one horrible moment she was afraid that the strength in her locked legs would give out, that they would both fall, tumbling head over heels to their deaths. Dizzy and sickened, with pain shooting up from her arm and shoulder, she hung upside-down and maintained her clutch on the boy's wrist with all her might.

'Dear God in heaven!' Matt's exclamation was shaken.

Tears streamed from her eyes and blinded her, for the boy's weight was too much. Her intake of breath was a tortured rasp. 'Help me!'

'Oh, darling—just hold on. I can almost reach him. Sian, for the love of God, don't slip now. Nearly there——'

A long, low moan broke from her lips as her entire body shook with the stress. Her torso was stretched in an intolerable bow, the tendons of her arm standing out like the strings of a violin keening. Then the weight eased, and Matt breathed, 'Got him. Let go!'

Her fingers slipped away strengthlessly. Tilting her head back, she watched with blurred, upside-down vision as he slung the boy on to his broad back, where Barry clung like a monkey. Matt looked up at her. The fear and tension had tautened the bones of his face into sharp angles before he started to dissolve into a white haze. All right now. Let go. Her lips parted in a sigh, and her dusky eyelashes fluttered.

'Sian!' Her name was a violent roar, and startled her alert. 'Don't faint! I'm going to hand him down to his mother and be right back. Don't move an inch—do you hear? Answer me!'

'I hear you,' she whispered, through the pounding in her head. She hurt all over, though, and shock was making her so dizzy. It would be terribly easy to just sleep ... she started to drift away on a spinning cloud ...

Until the warm, hard reality of Matt's hand eased underneath her abraded shoulders. He lifted her head and laid it gently in the hollow of his corded neck and shoulder, then slid his arm up and around her torso. 'There now, I've got you,' he soothed. 'You're safe. Try to put your arm around my neck and let go with your legs.'

She turned her face into the salted heat of his neck. She tried to put her injured arm around him but, though he felt so strong and rock-steady, she lacked capacity to

hold on to him. 'I can't do it,' she said in despair. 'I'll
fall.'

'Ssh,' he whispered, and turned his face into hers. The
corner of his open mouth moved against her cheekbone.
'I'd lose my arm before I let you fall. You'll just swing
around, that's all. I promise.'

Her weak tears slipped along his neck. 'But I've hurt
my shoulder. I don't think I can manage the climb down.'

'I'll be right behind you the whole way, with one arm
around your waist,' Matt said steadily. The rigidity of
his arm was severely restricting her breathing. 'Please,
Sian. Trust me.'

Her eyes closed, and she did as he asked, the tension
in first one leg, then the other, loosening in submission
to either death or safety. Her body swung around and
the world righted, and she groaned, a shaken animal
sound, at the terror and the pain of it. The muscles in
Matt's arm bunched hard as granite at her back; she
connected with the length of his body.

He had one leg hooked around a branch, the other
outstretched to a stronger one below, and he held her
perfectly steady with just the one arm—at what cost of
strength, she couldn't guess—until her feet had found
the same branch and she could stand for herself.

Then, for long moments, he just crushed her to him,
burying his face into her hair. 'I'll give you this much,
young lady,' he said tautly from the back of his throat,
'you do know how to frighten the wits out of a man.'

She huddled, shaking, between the barrier of his chest
and the tree trunk. 'Is he safe?'

'Safe and sound and howling his eyes out, the little
beast,' said Matt grimly. 'Sian, my love, delightful as it
is to hold you in my arms, I think could do a much

better job of it on the ground. Is this your way of sweeping me off my feet?'

She leaned her forehead on one hand. 'It was entirely unplanned, I assure you.'

'Your poor, lovely back—you're scraped all over. Have you the strength to hold on with one hand?' he asked. 'Good, then I want you to move as I move, and you can let go when I have my arm around your waist like this. All right?'

'All right.'

Pressed against her back, he bent to plant a swift kiss behind her ear. 'Good girl.'

The trip down to safety was a nightmare, made bearable only by Matt's steady chest pressed against her back. Afterwards Sian could never recall much of what happened; she just blindly put her hand and feet where he told her to, and trusted him to do the rest.

Then came the blessed moment when he helped her ease into a sitting position on the lowest, thickest branch before leaping gracefully to the ground. Sian leaned against the tree-trunk, scarcely able to believe that they had made it down alive.

There seemed to be quite a crowd around them, but such was her reduced state that the only person she had eyes for was Matt. Her huge, glazed eyes rested on him, numbly patient, until he straightened and turned back to her, the predator's gaze alien with relief and some vast undefineable emotion.

He held open his arms and said gently, 'Last stop, sweetheart.'

She went down into them as if she were coming home.

Sian woke with a start in darkness, and for a disorien-tated moment couldn't remember where she was or how

she had come to be there. Then, recognising the shape
and feel of her own bed and the familiar outlines of her
dresser in the moonlight that spilled in from half-shut
curtains, she relaxed and hugged a pillow to her chest.

The pillow was soft and had a faint, clean, spicy smell
to it that was strange and yet comfortingly familiar as
well. She turned her face into it, inhaling deeply. She
ached, all over, from the back of her knees along the
length of her raw back and stiff, sore shoulder, and the
throbbing lump at the back of her head.

Now she recalled the little boy stuck in the tree, though
the image was shot through with the recollection of fear
and pain, and through it all, stronger than anything,
threaded the memory of Matt's strong body.

After he had helped her down from the tree, he had
immediately swung her overstressed body into his arms
and carried her away through a babbling confusion of
thanks and well-wishing from the mother of the boy she
had helped to rescue. Sian had rested her aching head
against his shoulder, face turned into the privacy of his
neck.

Joshua and Steven were dispatched to clear away the
picnic things, while Jane came along to direct Matt back
to South Bend and the quickest route to Memorial
Hospital. Though the long day and the ride back had
made her sleepy, he wouldn't let her fall into a doze for
fear she had suffered concussion when she'd banged her
head.

At his and Jane's insistence during the speed-limit-
breaking drive, she had irritably recited times-tables,
poems, songs, anything that kept her awake and showed
she suffered no impairment of her faculties. Then came
the wait in the emergency ward, for X-rays and first aid.
The doctor who had seen her had been brisk and over-

worked; the heat, he had said, seemed to bring out all the crackpots, and he had looked at Sian as if she were one of them, while she tried to ignore Matt's sardonic smile and Jane's muffled chuckles.

Having found nothing wrong with her other than scrapes, bruises and strained ligaments, the doctor had prescribed some muscle relaxants for her stiffening arm and shoulder. Matt drove them back to the apartment and went to get the prescription filled, while Jane helped Sian bathe and dress in an over-long T-shirt.

When Matt had come back with the prescription, she'd swallowed a dose and had promptly gone out like a light, but she must have slept for hours, for the medicine had worn off and pain was what had awakened her.

The apartment was very quiet. Sian tried to twist around and find the luminous display of her bedside clock, and immediately wished she hadn't. It had just gone midnight, which meant that there was probably no one else around, for the group had been planning to see a midnight movie at the local cinema.

Because she was feeling under par and sorry for herself, Sian sniffed a bit and rubbed her nose into the fragrant pillow, and belated recognition blossomed as she recognised Matt's scent, which lingered on the linen case.

Of course, he had slept in her room only the night before. The smell of him triggered a whole wealth of images and it was no use trying to make sense of the convoluted and certainly stormy aspects of their relationship, for Sian's sensual memories were only of the good things—comfort, and strength, and the urgent relief with which he had held her after the traumatic ordeal.

Easy tears filled her eyes and she blinked them away angrily. All he had to do was be useful in a crisis, and

she started to associate his scent with attributes like re-
liability and steadfastness! She hadn't even known him
for more than a couple of days, and now, just because
she was feeling a little down and he had been there when
she had needed him, she had to go and miss him, didn't
she?

How sillily she was behaving, how weak and stupid!
This was just the sort of thing she had wanted to avoid:
this empty, idiotic yearning. Thank God she was too
sensible to fall in love with the man, for that would be
the final straw.

Oh, how she ached. Sian tossed and turned fretfully
but couldn't get into a position that gave relief to her
abused body. Finally having to admit defeat, she threw
back her covers and rose shakily on sore feet to search
for the muscle relaxants. If she remembered correctly,
Jane had left the bottle on the kitchen counter.

Sian left her bedroom and stepped into the hall. She
noticed the light was on in the living-room and curiously
went to investigate, for the light she and Jane normally
left on when they went out for the evening was the one
over the back porch.

As she limped around the corner and into golden, indirect illumination and the sound of soft music playing
on the stereo, a tawny head lifted from the arm of the
sofa where a long, tough body reclined, and Matt said
quietly, 'Sian?'

She faltered to a halt. One self-conscious hand crept
up to her gleaming, tousled hair as she asked in a sleep-
blurred voice, 'What are you doing here?'

'We felt that somebody should stay to keep an eye on
you in case you needed anything, and, as I'm not a
Monty Python fan, I volunteered,' he replied, rising
smoothly to his feet. He had forsaken his denim shorts

for a pair of equally faded jeans and grey sweat-shirt with the sleeves ripped off. His casual good looks and masculine presence were such an exactly perfect product of wish-fulfilment that the weak tears flooded back again and glittered brilliantly in her green eyes. 'What's the matter—feeling achy?'

The gentleness in the question was just what she had not needed. She turned away from him in embarrassed confusion as the tears spilled over, nodding mutely.

He walked around the edge of the sofa and put a careful arm around her. 'Come on. Let's get you some medication.'

She allowed herself to be led back through the hall, flinching and wiping her damp cheeks when he flicked on the light, but he never so much as glanced at her as he went to run cold water into a tall glass and shook out a couple of pills into his palm.

He offered them to her and she took them with a grimace, drinking thirstily until the water was gone. Then she exclaimed with disgust, 'I hate taking those things, they make me so dopey!'

His grin was keen and white as he took away the glass and set it in the sink. 'I know what you mean. Once I had whiplash from a car accident and took some, but I only ended up doing more injury to myself by walking into walls. Still, they'll help you sleep for the first couple of nights. Your bruises are coming up lovely, aren't they?'

She glanced down in even deeper embarrassment at the rainbow of colours mottling her bare arms. Some odd impulse made her say slowly, 'They look worse than they really are. I bruise very easily, and never remember afterwards how I managed to do it.'

The silence in the kitchen was very deep. Sian kept her face half averted, downbent. When Matt spoke, his voice was wry. 'Forgiveness, Sian?'

A violent tremor rippled through her. She waited until it passed. 'I don't know.'

'Your delicate skin——' He ran a light finger up her arm, then said abruptly, 'Why don't you come into the living-room with me until those muscle relaxants start to work, or are you already sleepy?'

She shook her head. 'I couldn't sleep yet.'

'All right,' he said easily, and opened up the refrigerator door. 'Want another cold drink? I'm having a beer, but I'm afraid that's out for you. What about orange juice?'

'Yes, please.' She watched him pour it, then asked somewhat awkwardly, 'How are you—any lasting effects from this afternoon?'

His mouth whitened as it drew tight and deepened the lines beside it. He let her precede him back towards the living-room. 'Not unless you count the aftermath of shock. I thought only near-death experiences were supposed to make one's life flash before one's eyes, but when I saw that kid start to tumble, and you lunged forward to grab him and it looked as if you were going to fall as well, all kinds of "should have beens" and "might have beens" flashed in front of me.'

'I didn't have anything like that,' said Sian with a frown as she curled stiffly on to the couch and he settled beside her. 'All I remember seeing after I fell back and hit my head was stars.'

'Yes, well,' he said, looking at her with an odd, grim expression that eased as he gave her the juice and opened his beer. 'You did a very courageous thing today, and at least we all survived to talk about it.'

Sian tilted back her head and drank, then afterwards regarded Matt's profile contemplatively. He was certainly unstinting in praising her for her courage, but in all honesty she had not really considered herself to be in any personal danger; when she had grabbed on to Barry's wrist, she had done so instinctively, without thought to the consequences such an action might possibly have for herself.

Real courage, or so it seemed to her, was what people like Matt possessed, for she knew that he had climbed far higher than was safe for a man of his size and weight, in full knowledge of what he risked. Yet he had made everything seem so easy, and not once spoken of what must have gone through his mind as he met her eyes in the tree and made his decision to act as he had. All his comments were of the fear he had felt for her sake, and the boy's, never his own.

'I owe you my life,' she said, not fully comprehending until that moment the truth in her words.

His head turned, a quick, startled movement. She was obscurely glad that he did not pass off her statement with a shrug and a flippant reply, for she was genuinely moved and the depth of her feelings could not be dismissed lightly.

'That little kid owes you his,' Matt said, with a slow, crooked smile. 'And the reckless, self-destructive boy I used to be owes the salvation of his to the memory of a wise girl who taught him the meaning of sanity, and quality of life. That's just how life is, Sian. That's the real message in your interlocking circles. You can't talk of *owing* anybody as if it were a debt to be paid. Our humanity binds us together with ties of decency, dedication and sometimes self-sacrifice. There isn't such a thing as a free spirit.'

She looked away, confused and troubled by what he'd said. It showed in the frown that drew the slim wings of her dark brows together.

'I'm not sure I agree with you,' she replied, and, though her gaze rested on the stereo across the room, what she saw in her mind's eye was the ghost of an abandoned, lonely little girl. 'My father's a free spirit who always does exactly as he pleases.'

'Does he?' Matt asked, settling back to put one long arm with extreme care along her shoulders. He stretched out his muscular legs. 'I don't know much about him, except that he cuts a rather exotic figure in Joshua's eye. He's quite a gambler, isn't he?'

'Yes,' she said drily, 'he's one of the best in the world. When I haven't been at boarding schools or university, I've been visiting him at whatever five-star hotel happens to be his home at the moment.'

The hand from the muscular arm circling her very gently tucked a black strand of hair behind her hair, making the moment into a caress. 'You must have been a beautiful little girl,' he said. 'I can just see you in a pretty dress, with your hair curling down your back and those huge, melting green eyes. If I had a daughter like that, it would break my heart to send her away.'

'Would it?' she asked, her throat aching. If Matt gave to his children the same profound gentleness that he had just now showed to her, he would be an excellent father. She almost found herself envying the woman who would become his wife.

'Yes. I also know,' he continued after a pause, 'that if I were in a job or lifestyle that was unsafe or unsuitable for that precious little girl, I would send her away, to some place where she could grow up safe, and I would deny myself the selfish pleasure of letting her depend on me too much. I can't speak for your father, of course, but self-sacrifice comes in many different ways.'

'Oh, you're right, of course,' she said with a sigh, as she leaned her tired, sore head back. The muscle behind her was very still. 'I know he does love me in his own fashion, and he did keep me with him as long as he possibly could. I certainly have never wanted materially for anything. I just want something better for my children, that's all. A real home where they can be happy, always knowing that they'll have some place to come back to if they need it. Is that too much to ask?'

'No,' he whispered, pulling her against his chest. 'That's not too much to ask.'

The muscle relaxants were working, and the throbbing pain in her limbs was liquidly melting away. She yawned so widely her jaw cracked, and drowsily considered asserting her independence by pushing away from him. In fact, she would in a minute.

Her head sank down to rest on his shoulder, and he shifted so that she could curl comfortably into his side. Warmth stole over her; who would have thought that the towering, icy stranger who tore strips off her at the party on Sunday would be such a delight to cuddle?

'Isn't it funny?' she murmured.

Matt rubbed his cheek against the perfumed softness of her hair, a slight, stealthy movement, and asked, 'Isn't what funny?'

'All the roles we play,' she murmured, and fell asleep.

He sat for a long time with his head bent down to hers, then, when headlights flashed through a gap in the curtains, he twisted unhurriedly to ease her lax body into his arms. She stirred to nestle her face into his sweatshirt but didn't rouse as he carried her into her room to tuck her into bed. For a few moments he stood looking down at the madonna-like beauty of her moonlit face until the voices of the returning cinema-goers sounded at the back door.

Then he bent, and pressed his warm mouth lightly against the luscious, still curve of her lips, and whispered, 'Wake soon, sleeping princess.'

Sian smiled and snuggled deeper into her pillow. She was dreaming of a midnight lover.

CHAPTER FIVE

THE phone was ringing as Sian fitted her key into the lock at the back door. She tried to hurry, but the mountain of bags and packages that she'd balanced precariously on one arm slowly listed to one side. Jane, similarly laden, lurched forward to catch them but they cascaded all around her.

Sian hesitated, caught between the mess on the porch step and the distant shrill of the phone, until Jane cried, 'Go on—go on—I'll pick all this up. It might be somebody important!'

She hurried down the hall as fast as her protesting muscles would allow, swung around the corner and lunged for the receiver. After all her scrambling, it would probably be for Jane, she thought in amusement, as she snatched up the handset and said breathlessly into it, 'Hello?'

There was a click and a crackle, then a man's voice, wonderfully familiar, came down the line, 'Sian?'

'Daddy!' she exclaimed in surprise and pleasure, as she dropped into a nearby stuffed chair.

'Sure, and what other man would be calling for you, darling?' Devin said teasingly. 'Might there be some little secret that you've been keeping from your old Dad?'

'Quite a few, now that I come to think of it,' she retorted with a grin, while a delighted glow spread all over her. He never failed to make her day when he called; she was crazy about him, fool that she was. 'But nothing along those lines. How are you? *Where* are you?'

He paused, but she must have imagined it, and promptly put the reason down to long distance when he said, 'London. I was just checking to see if your birthday present had arrived yet.'

'Yes, thank you,' she replied, touching the heavy antique gold necklace that she wore. It appeared deceptively plain but the craftmanship was exquisite, of Egyptian design, the smooth sculpted plates linked on the underside. The necklace had arrived by courier and was accompanied by a heavy cream card on which was the name of a company of an English insurance company, and must have cost a fortune. 'It arrived a few days ago, and it's simply gorgeous. I love it very much—I hardly ever take it off. Jane's threatening to take a pair of metal-cutters to it.'

'How is the little scamp?'

'She's fine. She's still wondering when you're going to take her ballroom dancing.'

'Well, you can tell her for me that the answer's still the same: not until she's grown an inch or two. I'm too old to get done for child molesting.'

'Forty-six isn't old!' Not that he even looked his age. With his elegant slim figure, unlined face and just a sprinkle of distinguished grey at the temples of otherwise jet-black hair, Devin Riley could easily pass for ten years younger. She could just picture him at seventy, leonine and gracefully light on his feet, charming his grandchildren with the same fairy-tales he used to tell her when she was small.

'It's old enough, daughter, it's old enough. So, tell me what you've been doing with yourself.'

Sian obligingly settled back and regaled him with various anecdotes from the last few weeks. She stifled a pang when she described the graduation ceremony he had not been able to attend, concentrating instead on his roar of laughter as she told him of the scene in which she dumped a laden plate down the front of a guest at the recent party, and how he grew silent over the incident about rescuing the little boy from the tree the day before yesterday, even though she took care to edit out the frightening bits.

Without bothering to explain that the party guest and Matthew were one and the same, she finally concluded, 'Joshua's older brother has invited us to his place in Chicago for the weekend, then it's down to work for those who have summer jobs. I've already said that I couldn't go to Chicago with the others since you're flying in for a visit. Do you have any idea how long you can stay?'

Again there was a pause, and Sian was sure she hadn't imagined it this time as it was such a lengthy one. 'That's another one of the reasons why I called, actually,' he told her. 'I'm afraid that I won't be able to come after all.'

'Oh, Da, no,' she said, unable to help herself as crushing disappointment settled on to her shoulders. First her commencement ceremony, then her birthday, and now this.

'I know, poppet. I wanted to be there as well, but it can't be helped.'

'But why ever not?' she asked, and hated herself for the asking. How many times over the past had they enacted the same scene? How many times did she tell herself that never again would she beg for his company, when it was obvious that he was too involved in his own life to make the time to share the important parts of hers? But this time, as ever, she had believed that things would be different. 'Surely if you've double-booked yourself, you could cancel your other engagements just this once?'

'I'm afraid not, darling.' The thread of disappointment that leadened the Irish lilt in his voice was really good, she thought bitterly. He could sound so sincere, so he could make her believe all over again, just when she'd erected her strongest barriers, that she was the most precious and important thing in the world to him.

'Well,' she said flatly, 'if it can't be helped, it can't be helped. Maybe next time, huh?'

'I'll be there with bells on, I promise. And in the mean time, there isn't a parent alive who could be more proud of their child than I am of you.'

'Yeah,' she whispered, opening her eyes very wide. But the tears spilled over anyway. 'Well, you tell Malcolm "hi" for me, will you? And tell him he'd better be looking after you. How is he, anyway?'

'Fine,' he said of his partner and old friend. 'Just fine.' He sounded so odd. 'Da, is anything wrong?'

'Of course not, poppet,' her father replied more strongly. 'We just have a bad connection.'

'All right, then. Take care of yourself.' But then, didn't he always?

'Sian——'

'Yes?' she asked, as he hesitated.

'Nothing,' he said with a sigh. 'I just love you, that's all.'

'I love you too, Daddy.'

And that, she thought coldly as she replaced the receiver, was the whole problem. Despite everything, she still loved her father.

Maybe love belonged to a secret society, a magical few who were imbued with the depth of personality that could cope with disappointment and disillusionment, then rise above them to emerge unscathed and without bitterness. Maybe there was some flaw in her that made her incapable of loving without clinging on.

She didn't know. But what terrified her enough to make her break into a cold sweat was that, if she could be so hurt by loving someone like her father, how much greater would be the pain if she were to fall in love with a man; really fall in love, with the complete and utter abandon that Matt had described that day on the beach?

She would never survive it. She hadn't the strength. An all-consuming passion like that would incinerate her to white ash; she knew it as she knew the force of her own emotions. She couldn't love a man and still keep her distance; she would give him her heart and soul until nothing remained of her but an empty shell.

Jane wandered back into the living-room, her relaxed demeanour dropping away instantly as she took in the sight of Sian's streaked, tight face. 'Who was on the phone?' she asked in quick concern.

Sian wiped her cheeks and tried to assume a more normal expression. 'It was my father. He isn't coming for the weekend after all.'

She could hardly bear the gentle look of compassion that came over her friend's face, and the disappointment for her sake. 'Oh, Sian, I am sorry.'

'Never mind,' she said, attempting a careless shrug. She thought she'd succeeded rather well. 'That's life.'

It might not be for some—for Matt. But that was how life was for her, and it was high time she got used to the fact and got on with it.

It had turned cooler, the sky leaden and overcast; the temperature had been so high over the weekend that by

Wednesday afternoon the sultry threat of thunderstorms was making Sian's head ache dully.

It suited her mood, which had turned grim and silent after talking with her father. Clad in jeans and sweat-shirt, she went out in the back garden to take advantage of the cooler weather while it held, weeding with scrupulous care the flower-bed she'd planted and maintained over the last four years.

After she'd finished a section, she sat back on her heels and stretched her aching back, dirt-encrusted hands lying passive in her lap. The moisture-heavy air was unrefreshing. She closed her eyes and tilted back her face, mouth tight with unhappiness. Just rain, damn it.

'You missed a weed,' said Matthew.

She started violently, heart thumping a wild rhythm, and her eyes flew open; she hadn't heard him approach. 'Think of the devil,' she said, deadpan.

His regard of her was sardonic, unsmiling. 'Always a dangerous thing to do.'

He stood at ease, balanced lightly as a swordsman, long legs planted a few feet apart, the thick, powerful thigh muscles straining the denim that covered them. He looked ready to hold his position forever if need be, or to pounce with lightning speed.

Sian ducked her head from the poised, lithe sight of him. She located the weed he had mentioned and yanked it, with a vicious twist of the wrist. Instead of pulling out the roots, it snapped in her clawed fingers. 'I thought you went back to Chicago,' she said, and could have groaned at what he might read into the flat statement.

'No. Vacation, remember?' said Matt briefly. He broke out of his fighter's stance, fluid as a dance, and crouched lightly beside her. 'I went to Indianapolis for the day, to visit my mother. Have dinner with me.'

Sian's soft mouth would have trembled, if she'd let it. She moved to another unweeded section, away from him. 'No.'

Matt's voice was harsh, impatient. 'Why not?'

'I'm busy.' She attacked another weed, shoulders hunched.

There was a pause, then he said, very evenly, 'Jane and Steven are going out tonight. Joshua is studying for his LSAT exams. What are you busy with?'

'None of your business.' She was very rude. She didn't care.

He did. Hard fingers snaked under her downbent chin and forced her face up, angry predator's eyes raking over her, raking through her tight façade with one neat, psychic claw-slash, and uncovering the pain beneath it. The harsh planes and angles of his face eased somewhat, as did his grip; she took advantage of that and jerked away, her breathing unsteady.

She thought he was going to comment on what he'd seen, but he didn't. Instead, Matthew rocked back on his heels and said, slow and contemplatively, 'Lobster bisque, sautéd scallops, chicken tetrazzini. Barbecued ribs, stuffed potato skins, linguini with shrimp, fried mushrooms. Fruit, yoghurt, salad, hell's bells, even a hamburger would do. Sian, I'm hungry.'

She had started to smile somewhere in the middle of his recital, albeit reluctantly, and at the pure pathos at the end she had to laugh out loud. At the musical sound the golden man kneeling beside her smiled, keen and white. She caught the tail end of it, just a suggestion of movement that drew her attention to the tough, sexy mouth. Her eyes lingered, helplessly fascinated in spite of herself, then she tried to cover it up by glancing down the robust, healthy length of him. 'You're obviously pining for a good meal,' she said wryly.

'So come oblige me,' he told her in prompt reply. 'Besides, I need to talk to you.'

'What are we doing now, chopping liver?' she parried with false lightness.

Jane called from the back porch, 'Hi, Matt. Anyone interested in a glass of lemonade?'

His hazel eyes held hers; they could contain a vast amount of patience when he willed it. 'Alone,' he added drily.

Sian wavered under his unrelenting stare, under Jane's growing curiosity; she didn't have anything planned for that evening, and she wouldn't put it past her blonde friend to confess as much to Matt. Oddly, instead of feeling trapped into acceptance, she felt lighter instead. 'All right,' she said in abrupt capitulation. 'Dinner.'

He rose to his feet immediately, a fluid surge of motion, and turned away even as she accepted; he would never be still for too long, for he was a creature of light and fire, a burning pillar who knew how to dampen the flaming inferno to accommodate the frailties of the company around him, but never quite extinguish it.

'I'll pick you up at eight o'clock,' said Matt over his shoulder. The slant of his gaze touched on her, with delicate amusement. 'Don't dress for a burger bar, will you? I'm not that desperate!'

Sian and her room-mate had to share the bathroom with courtesy and timing as they readied for their respective evenings, a ritual that had been perfected over the tenure of shared occupancy.

Sian wore an elegant cream linen suit and matching court shoes, with a long skirt that flowed to her shapely ankles. Her dull-mushroom blouse was pure silk, and the gold necklace winked with rich colour at the slim base of her throat. With her gleaming hair pulled back into a smooth French twist and her make-up subtly emphasising the contours of her green eyes and high cheekbones, she looked cool and composed, and strikingly elegant.

Jane was finished with the bathroom, so Sian nipped in to insert one last pin into her hair. When at last she was satisfied that the thick, heavy mass wasn't about to spill out of its confines in the middle of dinner, she swept up her cream bag and strolled to the open front door where Jane stood.

The calibre of the deep male voice was unmistakable. Jane and Matt were involved in their conversation, and so did not see Sian's stride falter, or the flustered flush that washed over her ivory complexion.

The rest of her afternoon had passed in a daze, but now with its dissipation came the mocking-bird cry that she must have been mad to consider going out with Matt for the evening. His presence was overwhelming enough in safe company; being alone with him, with the promise of languid hours spiralling ahead, carried the acrid scent of dynamite.

It was too late to back out. She recovered herself quickly enough, and by the time she reached the other two she appeared as unruffled as ever.

Dressed in a navy blue suit with a white shirt and tie, and gold cuff-links glinting at his strong wrists, Matthew looked formally elegant and impacted on the senses with the same breathtaking force as the first glimpse of a masterpiece painting. Sian's experienced eye admired the cut and rich quality of the suit and how it moulded itself without ostentatiousness and yet with devastating effect to the vibrant, powerful form of the body underneath.

Jane had paused in the middle of a sentence when the blonde saw that Matt's attention had shifted away from her, and an arrested expression had crept into his eyes. Sian looked up from the gleaming tips of his Italian shoes to his handsome face, and saw that he had caught her absorbed inspection. Neither Matt nor Sian responded to Jane's discreet goodbye as she left them alone.

His smile was naked and primitive, a lean, sexy, dangerous look that made Sian fear, shakenly, that she might be the main course for dinner.

'My God, a woman ready, and on time,' purred Matthew, as he leaned one expensively sheathed broad shoulder against the doorpost, in a negligent attitude that Sian could sense was utterly false. Underneath he was thrumming, the hunter held under flawless control. 'It's a gift a man would sell his soul for.'

Whatever had wound him up, Sian would, for sanity's sake, have to quell. She said, imperturbable and prosaic, yet with wary eyes, 'Surely there's no need for such an extreme, when the price of a well-cooked dinner will suffice.'

'Madam,' said the devil who was a gentleman, with a deceptively submissive inclination of his tawny head, 'I assure you, I am entirely at your service.'

His wicked gaze held hers, managing to make what would otherwise be an innocuous reply into something smokily suggestive. Sian felt a hot, betraying tide of colour rise to her cheeks. He saw, and his smile widened just a taunting fraction, and her composure broke.

'You need to be put on a leash!'

'What an evocative fantasy,' he murmured. 'Do you see your hand at the other end?'

Her nostrils flared in a hissing inward breath. He was incorrigible in his present mood. She almost turned back, and be damned to courtesy. Almost, but she stepped off the threshold and into the night, her narrow hands white on her bag, racketing heart in her throat, the pain and disappointment from that afternoon quite forgotten.

'I'd be far too wise to want to hold your leash,' she said, green eyes flashing at brilliant odds with her even tone. 'Headstrong as you are, I'd only gain whiplash for my pains.'

'You disappoint me,' murmured Matt, his hand a hot brand through the material of her jacket as he led her to the Mercedes. 'From our conversation on the beach two days ago, I would have said that control held all the attraction for you.'

'You misunderstood,' she replied, carefully, delicately feinting. She slid into the seat, soft leather whispering a sigh as her weight settled in the bucket seat. 'I only ever desire control over my own destiny, never over another human being.'

'Ah,' he replied, one corner of his mouth curled, as he eased into the driver's seat. 'A chill, polite distance between you and the rest of the world. What a lonely life you have ahead of you.'

'Your point of view,' she said, with a supreme gentleness that only afterwards did she realise sounded like a goad. He drove them swiftly, expertly along the route to a reputable restaurant, while a reckless glitter shone in those hazel eyes and an emotion akin to anger tautened the skin across hard cheekbones.

Thinking to divert whatever riotous intention impelled him, she licked dry lips and asked, 'What was it you wanted to talk to me about?'

He shot her a glance from under slanted brows, but remarked with cool apparent irrelevance, 'Jane told me that your father couldn't come for the weekend.'

The reminder made her calm expression flicker, a brief crack in the poised façade that hardened into rigidity. 'That's right,' she said, obsessively neutral.

Perhaps he had missed it. He continued, 'That means you could come to Chicago with the other three.'

He was indifferent, extending a courtesy forced on him by extenuating circumstances. She said, watching him, 'Only if you have the room to put up one more person.'

Now he seemed surprised at her cautious diffidence. 'Well, of course. You were included in the invitation to begin with. I'm sorry for your sake that your father couldn't make it, but his loss is our gain. Do you fancy going to the theatre on Friday night, or will that be a bit much after the drive?'

'I can't speak for the others, but I'd love to,' she said slowly, still in part reserved because of his apparent change of mood and yet disarmed at the importance he seemed to attach to her opinions and wishes.

'Then I'll have a look around tomorrow and see what I can book. We can go to supper afterwards, and, if we're out during the day on Saturday, I thought I'd invite some people over for the evening. Then you can sleep as late as you like the next morning, have a relaxing brunch with the Sunday papers, and travel back to South Bend at your leisure. That way those of you who have summer jobs lined up won't be too tired on Monday. How does that sound?'

It sounded carefully thought out, and considerate, and just exactly right. The last of her lingering disappointment, which had been resurrected by the topic of conversation, faded away as she began to look forward to the weekend.

'Well done,' she said quietly. 'But your plans can't
have been what you wanted to discuss. You didn't know
this afternoon that my own plans had fallen through.'

The Mercedes slid into a parking space at the restaurant. Matthew turned off the engine and turned to
her, his expression inscrutable. 'No, I didn't,' he said
softly, 'did I?'

The confinement of the car was stifling. Sian un-
buckled her seatbelt as quickly as her fumbling fingers
would allow, but he must have had split-second reflexes,
for he was already striding around the back of the convertible to reach her door even as she grasped the handle.
What she had intended as an escape became an ad-
vancement into further confrontation, as she slid long
legs around and rose to her feet.

The added height from her heels brought her almost
to his level. The fact added a subtle link in her armour;
Sian didn't like the vulnerability she felt when she had
to tilt back her head to look up at him.

'Well, then,' she said at last, obscurely disturbed by
his coiled manner and his reticence, 'what was it?'

Matthew's amusement was a dangerous, velvet thing.
'Did no one ever tell you about curiosity and the dead
cat?'

Her nostrils pinched. She told him, with a pointed
chill as he curled one hand around her elbow and they
strolled towards the restaurant, 'You were the one to in-
itiate this. I was merely following through.'

'Yes, tenacity is one of your strong points, isn't it?'
He shouldered a door open and slanted a smile at her,
brief and private. 'I would do well to remember that.'

She chose to ignore what his intense regard did to her
midsection, and stepped into warmth, light and muted
noise.

Sian had heard of the restaurant but had never been. She liked the rich wood décor and the unobtrusive efficiency of the staff. As the hostess checked for Matthew's booking, then led them to their table, she wondered, surprisingly without much heat, just when he had made the reservation. Before or after he had talked with her? But then perhaps he had meant to eat here whether she came or not. She was glad she had not said something precipitate and foolish.

She could not help but be aware of the attention they received, in an oblique fashion, from the other diners in the restaurant as they walked through. Sian saw the women glance casually at Matthew's sulphurously graceful prowl, then halt in wide-eyed assessment. One or two held forks suspended in mid-air. She had a sudden, primitive image of stalking over to the more blatant ones and slapping their laden utensils out of their hands.

When Matthew held out a chair, she settled into it smoothly, her face dark with self-mockery.

Their conversation was at first desultory as they perused the menu. Sian settled quickly for a simple meal of grilled rainbow trout, salad and a glass of white wine. Matt ordered a steak, then when their waiter left he settled back in his chair and lazily contemplated her. What shifted, she wondered, behind those private eyes, reflecting the intense blue of his dark suit so that he seemed almost a stranger?

'What will you be doing with your summer, Sian?' asked Matt, one corded, long-fingered hand idly twirling the glass of Scotch that had been set before him. 'Do you have a job lined up?'

'I was going to wait until my father came for his visit before I decided what to do,' she replied, unaware of her wry grimace or the downward bent of her mouth. 'Now I suppose I'll have to rethink things. To be quite honest, I'm not sure what I'll do. The last few months of school have been too pressured for me to do anything but cope with the deadlines as they came up.'

'Jane mentioned you graduated top of your class. Congratulations,' he said, 'and well done. You've worked very hard.'

'Thank you.' Her green eyes held genuine pleasure from his praise. 'But it's not over yet.'

Their meal came, attractively displayed and superbly cooked. Sian picked at hers without much interest.

'You're going on to graduate school?' he asked after the interruption.

'Mmm, two more years.' He was not looking at her any longer, but instead studied the amber lights in his drink; she wasn't sure why she went on to confess, slowly, 'I'm rather intimidated by it, actually. Courses in business administration aren't exactly my strong point.'

'So you choose to grapple with the subject, instead of avoiding it. I'm sure you'll do just fine once you're in the middle of it,' he remarked. His iced-water glass was sweating. With one forefinger he wiped down the edge of the glass and came away wet. She gave the movement close attention. Matt lifted his gaze and said softly, 'After all, as with anything else, it's the anticipation that's the worst part.'

The gold necklace at the base of her neck winked with her tight swallow. 'Is it?' she said very drily, regarding him from under level brows. 'And what of reality that exceeds all expectations?'

He was sober-faced, and laughing at her. 'Clarify the matter for me. I don't see reality's exceeding all expectations as necessarily a terrible thing.'

'Catastrophe?' she murmured. Her sarcasm was a delicacy flavouring her words with rare spice. 'Flood, fire, act of God?'

'One cannot live one's life in constant fear of disaster, Sian,' he returned. 'Bad things do happen, to good and bad people alike. Don't you see that's why it's so important to snatch at the good when fortune presents it to us?'

Her smile was excessively mild. 'I don't disagree with you, Matthew. I do, however, take issue with the imposition of your values over mine. I'm the one to judge what's good in my life, and I will take it where I find it.'

His face had tightened until it was a study in angled severity. It gave her no pleasure to look on it. 'Like Joshua?' he bit out.

She lifted her chin. She didn't know why she didn't just either tell him she was 'engaged' to his brother, or confess the real story to him. The timing would have been right for either. But one was a weapon she wasn't prepared to use, and the other too revealing. 'If I choose,' she said coolly.

His eyes glittered. She distrusted him, and her own assessment of his strange mood, however, as he paid for their meal with apparent composure, as they strolled leisurely to the parking area.

She did well to be wary, but it was not enough. She waited in silence while he unlocked her door, then quelled an impulse to step back as he straightened and turned to regard her with brooding eyes, a taut mouth.

'I have been remiss. I never did tell you how lovely you look,' Matthew said then, almost absently. 'You are stunning, Sian. I was proud to be seen by your side tonight.'

She was shaken by the intensity of pleasure that coursed through her at his quiet compliment. How vain she was, to know such a fierce thrill at his words, and to know, too, that they had been judged well matched by outsiders: her cool femininity in delicate contrast to his forceful masculinity.

'Thank you,' she said, gravely, sternly demure.

He looked down her, a bright and graceful fall. They stood in relative privacy between the passenger side of the Mercedes and the car parked next to it. The light from a nearby street-lamp burned white along the edge of his bent tawny head; the rest of his face was in translucent shadow.

'I like your blouse.'

An irony: despite the intimacy of his regard, she had room to be grateful that he wasn't looking at her face, which felt as if it were glowing neon-red. Her throat needed to be cleared before she could speak. 'I like it too.'

He asked throatily, tightly, 'Is it as soft and as silken as it looks?'

Her legs went wobbling. She said, shaken and alarmed, 'I don't think——'

He brought a hand up inside her open suit jacket and slid the fingers around the slim curve of her ribs, just under her breast, and at the light caressing pressure her pulse went wild.

'Mmm,' he sighed, with deceptively sleepy pleasure. 'It is. Cool and whispery thin, and moulding itself to the body underneath it. That's how a woman should always dress, in silk and lace, and—well, maybe a touch of leather.'

His hand moved to the small of her back, and he pulled her to him, and with slow, sensuous deliberation he began to lower his head.

Her composure, so hard won at the beginning, so grimly maintained throughout the evening, was now a quivering bowl of jelly. It trembled strengthlessly at the pit of her stomach, at the back of her knees, in the base of her throat, and the softened curve of her mouth. 'Matthew,' she managed to gasp. 'Stop it.'

His lips hovered, a bare inch from hers. 'I'm sorry, I don't understand,' he murmured with oh, such false innocence, as he lifted molten eyes. 'That isn't the message your body was telling me on the beach.'

Her hands rested on his forearms, tightened convulsively on him. Her lips had gone dry; she licked them and whispered, 'It's what I'm telling you now.'

With her body bowing back against the strength of his arm, her eyes dilated to immense black pools; she looked young, dazed and blinded. He took his time in examining her face, the arced lines of her collarbones as they disappeared in shadowed mystery into the neck of her blouse. Then he shook his head a little, and said softly, 'No, you're not.'

Her eyelids fell under an unsustainable weight as he kissed her, a featherlight, moulded, exploratory caress, and the same searing judder of sensation that always happened when he touched her crackled down the length of her body. She made some slight sound, reactive, incoherent, and his whisper of expelled breath answered.

Gentleness, civilisation's veneer, was discarded for the game it was. He took her fully into his arms, hard against the length of him, and slanted his opened mouth over hers.

The dark, secret invasion was impossible to resist. Her lips parted on a sigh. He touched her inside, drew her out, and danced with her tongue. She whirled mindlessly in a downward spiral, head to one side and sinking fast to his shoulder, moulded breast to hard-muscled breast, the arc of hip to hip, thigh to thigh.

She felt it as if it shook her own foundations, the uncontrollable tremor that raced over him like fever. He cupped the back of her head, then dug with delicate urgency into the French twist until the pins scattered away and her hair spilled over her shoulders and he sank greedy fingers into the midnight rain.

If he had not been holding her so very tightly, she would have slid down to the ground. As it was, she clung to him, her arms wound around his neck by some mysterious force while common sense flew away on fickle wings and he drove with hard, escalating passion into her unplumbed depths.

His heart beat like a sledge-hammer against her breasts. His breath was coming in long-distance-runner gasps; gradually he eased the ferocity of the tempo into something more bearable, swooping with shallower intent on the bruised peach of her mouth. If it was meant to soothe and restore, it did the exact opposite. Plunged into the dazzling, uncloaked sexuality of the former kiss, then offered this, was like denying a condemned man his last meal, and she trembled with a violent gnawing hunger she'd never before experienced, nor knew how to assuage.

At last he turned his head away with a sharp, muffled sound, and pressed her face not gently—not that—into his neck. They stood thus for some minutes, in reverberative silence too tense for words, while he stroked her hair and back.

Sian was suffering from deep, uncomprehending shock. She felt as if she had lived all her life with blinkers on, like some kind of ironic joke: I see, said the blind man, as he picked up his hammer and saw. Or that the world of colours and textures that she loved so much had suddenly sprouted a fourth dimension. There was no room in her for the concept that had just exploded all around her, and inside her, with the force of nuclear fusion. She couldn't recover because she didn't know where she had been.

Then Matthew stirred, and sighed into her hair, and said hoarsely, 'That's what you were saying to me.'

She shook her head dumbly. She didn't know what she was doing. One hand threaded in her hair clenched into a powerful fist. 'You lack proof?'

Even his growl was an invasion; it permeated her body. She breathed hard once, in distress, and would have shaken her head again. She could not. She was trapped, by his hands and by the truth.

'Matthew,' she whispered, violently unsteady, 'you push me too far.'

His head reared back, the ferocious male gaze narrowed, that tight evocative mouth twisted. 'I, push you?' he breathed, a visual and audible statement of incredulity. 'Woman, you don't know what you're talking about. Look at you—every aspect about you is a provocation. Your mouth, your skin, those high, firm breasts, and curving hips were made for ravishment, and you lock it all away in a safe pretence and a polite distance, and a stubborn belief for the future you know will shrivel everything generous and giving inside you.'

'Shut up!' Her lovely face twisted. His hold at the back of her head, on her senses and crumbling convictions was making her crazy with pain and desire. She raised her hands to strike at him; she, who had never before done or wished to do violence to another human being in her life. Her fingers curled around the intransigent poles of his wrists, an ineffective shackle, an impossible protest as she strained to gain her freedom.

If anything he became even more reckless, a rampant wildfire that drove her, fleeing, before its devouring heat. 'I will not!' he snarled. Then, strangely, he opened his fingers and spread her raven hair along the palms. 'Oh, look,' said Matthew, 'I've messed up your lovely hairstyle. Somehow you don't look so cool and unapproachable any more, darling. Why, if anyone sees you this way, they'll think you've been *kissed*.'

She shook all over. It must be fury. It must. Her lips trembled as she struggled to hold it in, but the laughter stole like a thief from her anyway.

He froze, listening to her laugh, looking at her overbright, tear-glazed eyes. A toss up, between one or the other, and laughter had won. The thrumming tension in his body eased. He said ruefully, 'I've been abominable, haven't I?'

'Now and then,' she admitted. Her hair slipped, silken and elusive, from his fingers, and he stroked the sides of her face. She could have pulled away, for she was no longer held prisoner. She didn't. 'But perhaps I've goaded you.'

Matthew ran his thumbs over the crushed softness of her lips, and said, 'Now and then. Your hairpins flew everywhere, didn't they? Want me to collect them for you?'

He bent to the dirty asphalt, looked around, then cocked a doubtful eyebrow at her. 'Leave it,' she said, still laughing. 'You'll never find them all.'

Her cheeks were flushed, her green eyes vivid, her raven hair falling gloriously about her shoulders, and he rocked back on his heels to stare up at her.

'Sian, you take my breath away,' he said quietly.

Her laughter died, and what came in its place was chilled and fearful. 'Don't,' she whispered.

He rose until he towered above her, and her huge gaze rose with him. For a moment he looked stern, hard, a bedrock of the adamance that was always seen through the swirling mists of his ever-changing moods. She remembered the icy stranger she had met on Sunday, and shivered.

But then his grimness passed away, and he said, 'But to deny it would be to deny what has happened here between us, and I'm not prepared to do that. Come, I'll take you home.'

Well, she thought as she climbed into the car with a vague, secret, ever-to-be-denied sense of anticlimax, you couldn't really get more mundane than that.

DOUBLE YOUR ACTION PLAY...

"ROLL A DOUBLE!"

Peel off label & place inside

**CLAIM 4 BOOKS
PLUS A FREE
GIFT**

ABSOLUTELY FREE!

SEE INSIDE..

NO RISK, NO OBLIGATION TO BUY...NOW OR EVER!

GUARANTEED

PLAY "ROLL A DOUBLE" AND GET FIVE FREE GIFTS!

HERE'S HOW TO PLAY:

1. Peel off label from front cover. Place it in space provided at right. With a coin, carefully scratch off the silver dice. Then check the claim chart to see what we have for you – FREE BOOKS and a gift – ALL YOURS! ALL FREE!

2. Send back this card and you'll receive brand-new Harlequin Presents® novels. These books have a cover price of $2.99 each, but they are yours to keep absolutely free.

3. There's no catch. You're under no obligation to buy anything. We charge nothing – ZERO – for your first shipment. And you don't have to make any minimum number of purchases – not even one!

4. The fact is thousands of readers enjoy receiving books by mail from the Harlequin Reader Service® months before they're available in stores. They like the convenience of home delivery and they love our discount prices!

5. We hope that after receiving your free books you'll want to remain a subscriber. But the choice is yours – to continue or cancel, anytime at all! So why not take us up on our invitation, with no risk of any kind. You'll be glad you did!

©1990 Harlequin Enterprises Limited

You'll look like a million dollars when you wear this lovely necklace! Its cobra-link chain is a generous 18" long, and the multi-faceted Austrian crystal sparkles like a diamond!

NOT ACTUAL SIZE

"ROLL A DOUBLE!"

PLACE LABEL HERE

SCRATCH HERE

?

SEE CLAIM CHART BELOW

106 CIH ANEM
(U-H-P-03/94)

YES! I have placed my label from the front cover into the space provided above and scratched off the silver dice. Please rush me the free books and gift that I am entitled to. I understand that I am under no obligation to purchase any books, as explained on the back and on the opposite page.

NAME _____

ADDRESS _____ APT. _____

CITY _____ STATE _____ ZIP CODE _____

CLAIM CHART

		4 FREE BOOKS PLUS FREE CRYSTAL PENDANT NECKLACE
		3 FREE BOOKS
		2 FREE BOOKS

CLAIM NO.37-829

BUSINESS REPLY MAIL
FIRST CLASS MAIL   PERMIT NO. 717   BUFFALO, NY

POSTAGE WILL BE PAID BY ADDRESSEE

HARLEQUIN READER SERVICE
3010 WALDEN AVE
PO BOX 1867
BUFFALO NY 14240-9952

NO POSTAGE
NECESSARY
IF MAILED
IN THE
UNITED STATES

CHAPTER SIX

THE drive back to her apartment was undertaken in complete silence. By running her hands through her hair, Sian managed to restore at least some order, and her colouring had returned to its normal flawless cream.

The Mercedes turned gently on to her street. She stared out of the window, feeling the pressure build inside her head as the houses melted past. After the resounding clash from earlier, this nothingness, this total withdrawal, felt like a desolation. Dinner and a kiss? The inadequate description was unacceptably trite. What had it been, Sian? What?

Dinner, not a few kisses, and...

They pulled up to the apartment, and she was her own greatest fan, as she achieved a perfection of cool courtesy. 'Coming in for coffee?'

But Matthew was already out of the car and coming around to her side. 'So you decided to speak to me after all?' he remarked, one eyebrow slanted mockingly. 'And here I thought I was the recipient of a magnificent sulk. I don't know whether to be relieved or disappointed.'

He always managed instant ignition. She snapped, 'I don't sulk!'

The mockery became an outright laugh. She managed to fit her key in the back door lock and entered the cool dark kitchen, the hunter a close-following, silent menace. He found the light switch and snapped it on. She turned away from him, heard the echo of emptiness throughout the rooms. Oh, God. Get thee behind me, Satan...

She felt to the counter and drew the coffee-maker towards her, and asked severely, 'How many cups would you like?'

'I don't want any coffee,' said Matthew irritably.

How he tried her. She bowed her head over the machine while her teeth clenched, then she pushed away from the counter and turned to glare at him. He was a restless caged beast, prowling.

'I think this was a mistake,' she gritted. 'Maybe you had better go, before either of us does yet another thing to regret.'

'But Sian,' he purred, cocking that insolent brow at her, 'you haven't asked me what I do want.'

She closed her eyes, as liquid lightning bolted down her legs. 'No, I haven't,' she whispered, averting her pale face in sharp rejection. 'I don't want to know.'

'Always a contrary creature,' Matthew muttered, swinging with neat violence as he reached the limit of the kitchen, and turned to stalk back. 'I say black, she says white. I say wrong, she says right. Is this what it means to be a woman, Sian? Everything has to be bent, nothing straightforward, bluff and rebuff.'

His face was filled with dark enjoyment.

'Heaven give me strength,' she groaned. 'Can't we even have a simple civilised conversation? Why must everything be a battleground for you?'

'Oh,' he said with angry wisdom, *'that's* why you invited me in for coffee—a simple, civilised conversation. About the weather, perhaps? It would have to be something appropriately distant for you, wouldn't it? Containable, in control.'

'You're quite mad, you know,' she uttered, with the perfect calm of conviction. She was pressed back against the counter as if she would melt into the wood.

'No,' he replied grimly, 'but I am going crazy. I'll tell you what I want. I want to fight. I want a good, hard, rousing, no holds barred, nasty fight. Care to oblige me?'

'Be careful what you ask for,' she warned, hands curled into stiff claws at her sides.

He stuck his face into hers and snarled, 'I'm not finished yet.'

She met him thrust for thrust, furiously. 'I think you might wish to be!'

He swung away from her, on another pacing lap. It was not a retreat. 'Then,' he continued, as stark and as unrestrained as if she hadn't spoken, leaning his long, taut body against the table, 'we make up.'

She hadn't seen it coming and felt the breath knocked out of her. His hazel glare on her tell-tale face was insatiable. 'Push and shove, Sian,' he whispered roughly of the maelstrom primeval. 'Your angry spitting, and the limits of my endurance. I push you too far. You push me over the edge. How do you cushion a man who's falling? The fight's over now, and making up has a sweetness to pierce the soul.'

Her mouth shaped words, but the words had no sound, just the shape and the siren call of his name, plea and curse, and invocation.

'Then I would want you to walk over,' he muttered. His eyes closed. He tilted back his face, that harsh and worldly, compulsively handsome, predator's face. He leaned back on his hands, the suit jacket falling open to white-covered torso, the muscular legs outstretched and slightly splayed. 'Your grace of movement, green eyes intent with slumbrous warmth and the residue of fire. I would want you to come to me with confidence and surety. I would want you to catch me before I fall too far, with the feline ease of the slightest touch which is given in desire.'

He filled her vision, encompassed her world. He made the fight so seductive, she might never want to make love to another man. His serpent's tongue pulled her across the gulf of the floor, a whisper of movement between his legs. The convex breadth of his broad chest, tapering to slim waist, was a haven for her shaking fingers.

Her butterfly touch arced his body. It brought her down to him, curved her to fit the power of his offered bow. She fell victim tenderly without a sound, and her eyes closed, and her face lowered over his rigid mouth. At the meeting of her soft lips with his, he shuddered his delight and torment, and groaned, and sprang his sultry trap.

His arms closed around her, and he rose up from the table, and as he gained his full height he carried her up with him so that her feet left the floor and she was flush and heavy against him, an irrevocable strain, no holds barred. His mouth was a piercing, open furnace.

Her arms wound around his neck. The world moved and the light became intolerable. He was laying her on the table, his shoulders the bowl of the sky, spearing her wetness with his ravening tongue. Her thighs trembled and he parted them, and came between them as no one had ever done before, and his hardness pressed against her and made her own heat intolerable.

Then he reared back in shocking retreat, his entire body a scream of protest. 'Ah, goddammit, no.'

She felt flayed by a whip. Her eyes opened, searing in her blinded face, framed by his sheltering forearms and the snaking black beauty of her hair.

Matthew devoured her with his ferocious, loss-filled eyes. His naked face. She didn't understand.

Then she, too, heard it: the slam of car doors, familiar teasing voices, leisurely approaching footsteps, the advent of discovery. The comprehension of it slammed into her and twisted her expression into pure frustrated rage.

Matt hauled her to her feet in a dizzying wrench, shoved her to the hall and said savagely, 'Go to the bathroom.'

She went; somehow, she went.

With shaking hands she splashed cold water on her overheated face and throat, straightened her rumpled suit, found a comb and ran it through her hair. Then she looked at herself in the mirror.

Was this what he had seen—the dilated eyes gone brilliant and black and ringed with emerald? The flush on her high cheekbones that matched the crushed velvet of her mouth? She stared at the woman, who was a stranger.

When she was as presentable as she could possibly make herself, she left the bathroom and walked into the kitchen.

Jane had made the coffee that Sian had forsaken. Her blonde friend sat at the table with Steven, and Joshua, and, as the kitchen set had only four chairs, Matthew had appropriated a tall stool, leaving the fourth chair empty for her.

She stood unnoticed in the doorway and studied him numbly. That tough countenance was composed, shuttered, the lean body in that elegant suit relaxed. He looked distinctly undisturbed by the cataclysmic events that had just taken place, and she searched for hate in her terrified heart, for she had been cauterised.

Then she saw the dark residue of heat that clenched his skin, the hooded glitter of his eyes, and her hands, which had clawed, flexed.

Jane saw her first and smiled in puzzlement. 'Hi, did you have a good dinner? We rescued Joshua from his books. Sian, wasn't your hair...?'

Sian's eyes flashed at her, a brief warning flick. Her friend's voice died away. Suddenly Jane became very busy with serving coffee to everyone, while under the distraction of the movement Sian slid weakly into the empty chair beside Matthew, who looked at her with a tight, sulphurous smile.

'We rode to the restaurant with the convertible top down, and Sian's hair blew everywhere,' lied Matt smoothly, his tawny brows slanted mockingly. 'She still hasn't forgiven me for ruffling her feathers, have you, darling?'

Her heart thumped. Damn him, he should have remained silent and let Jane's remark pass into oblivion. Then, because everyone was looking at her for some kind of reply, she grimaced and said drily, 'I looked as if I'd been dragged through a bush backwards.'

Steven and Joshua laughed. Jane was staring at her profile; she could feel it and didn't dare to look at her friend, or her fixed, set expression would crumble. She took the only revenge she could on Matt, groping surreptitiously with her foot to grind her stiletto heel into the toe of his shoe.

She could feel his silent grunt as the conversation turned to other things, then he casually shifted his position, putting one hand on the back of the chair behind Sian's head while lifting his foot out of range.

It looked an elegant, indolent pose and also placed her into the half curve of his body. She tried to ignore the long, hard thigh pressing against her arm, but found it was a losing battle. She could feel every flex and shift of the muscle sliding underneath the dark cloth and in desperation she turned to chatter animatedly to the others.

She nearly leaped out of her skin when she felt the stealthy caress of his fingers flowing through the fine, sensitive hairs at the nape of her neck. Unseen by any of the others, the ball of his thumb found the base of her skull and rotated with sensuous gentleness against the soft skin, and her whole body quivered in response.

It was agony, trying to maintain a semblance of normality while wave upon wave of chaotic emotion clashed symphonic cymbals inside her so loudly that she was amazed no one else could hear it. Fury, sheer, inarticulate stupefaction at his audacity, and an insidious pleasure, warred for supremacy; and she could sense the tension weaving through his otherwise placid demeanour.

'Are you all right?' Joshua asked her. 'You look sort of dazed.'

Incautiously she said the first thing that came into her reeling head. 'Oh, I'm fine, I'll just be ready for bed soon.'

Her tormentor shook, a fine tremor that ran down his whole body, and oh, she could wish for the freedom to curse him to a thousand hells. She slipped one hand under the cover of her other arm, groped at his thigh until she had a good hold of skin and cloth and pinched as hard as she could.

'Ouch!' he snapped. He had to sit forward to jerk away, which thankfully removed the hand at her neck.

'What's wrong?' asked Jane, surprised.

'My leg went to sleep,' drawled Matthew, as he flexed the injured limb. His face was creased with sardonic amusement. 'It feels as if a cat has sunk her claws into it.'

'You ought to be more careful in how you position yourself in the future,' Sian said in a sugary voice and a poisoned smile.

He shot her a dark look and growled at her. 'You're an unsympathetic woman, Sian Riley.'

She clicked her fingers at him. 'Hard as nails, that's what I am.'

The other three became involved in some kind of argument. It sounded good-natured. Sian assumed an attentive expression and never heard a word of it. Matthew had hooked an ankle around one of her legs and slid down her calf slowly. Her mouth shook, and she pressed the offending tender flesh tight in desperation. He reached her shoe and began to ease it from her narrow foot.

She exploded upright. 'The air in here seems awfully stuffy,' she snapped, as four pairs of eyes regarded her, three of them surprised. 'I think I'll go change out of this suit.'

Matt turned his tawny head. They stood staring at each other for a brief moment, and she could feel his proximity like a coal brazier emitting heat. He murmured, *sotto voce*, 'Running away?'

'Just forming a strategic retreat until you start behaving yourself,' she replied grimly, proud of her even tone.

Neither of them cared about their fascinated audience. Matthew's eyes gleamed, satiric and lazy. 'How unutterably tame, sleeping princess.'

She thrust her angry expression close to his and said succinctly, 'The French call it etiquette. In case you were wondering, that stands for good manners. Excuse me, please.'

'Wait, Sian, I'll come with you. I just remembered I didn't put your clothes away after doing laundry today,' declared her friend, who scrambled to her feet in an untidy rush.

Sian stared at the blonde in amazement, for today had not been laundry day. But questions were beyond her; she pivoted on her heel and stalked out of the kitchen, her room-mate close behind.

As she travelled down the hall, she thrust her hands through her hair distractedly and held on to her head. It seemed that she and Matthew were destined to enter into a relationship that throbbed with disturbing undercurrents of one kind or another, which invariably built up to a static discharge of glowing white sparks.

First it had been his disapproval over Joshua's intended proposal. Now it looked as though he had every intention of niggling away at her peace of mind in an unrelenting pursuit of—Sian's mind shied away from the memory of what had happened in the restaurant car park, the kitchen, then she forced herself to be blunt to the point of crudity.

Face facts, she told herself fiercely. She had offered herself to him earlier, and he had only done what any normal, healthy male would have. Was it entirely his fault, considering that she had reacted the way she had?

She would have melted into a stunned heap at his feet had he let her. The gall of it—after all her fine philosophising about what she was looking for in a husband, about how she scorned passionate affairs of the heart, then one seductive touch from him and she flared like a torch.

So what did she think she was playing at, allowing herself to be seduced by him? What did he think to gain? Was she a challenge to him because of her differing standards, or merely light relief?

She had to come to some conclusion, and fast, because otherwise she would find she had trapped herself into another dangerous situation by emitting unconscious signals he was sure to pick up. Maybe it would be wisest just to cry off the weekend party at his place. Then she might never have to see him, or face his provocative unpredictability, again.

She strode into her bedroom, as did Jane, who shut the door behind her. Sian couldn't look at her friend. Instead she began to jerk her clothes off in tight, frustrated movements.

Jane had settled on her bed and after a moment asked, 'Are you going to tell me what's happened between you and Matt?'

Off came her suit jacket. Usually so neat, she threw it into a corner and slipped out of her skirt. 'What makes you think anything happened?'

'Because,' retorted her friend in exasperation, 'you two are sparring again as if World War III is about to break out!'

The skirt followed the jacket, then her blouse, and her shoes and tights. Sian's mouth was twisted in wry resignation. Trust Jane to barge right into the heart of the matter. Then, because she hated to hurt her friend's feelings and she needed someone to confide in anyway, she said as she yanked a T-shirt over her head, 'He kissed me.'

How inadequate were the words; but she couldn't confess the real depth of what had happened to save her life. Jane appeared disappointingly unsurprised. 'So? I'd already figured as much.'

She swivelled around to face her face and asked grimly, 'Was it that obvious?'

'Sweetheart, I know you,' replied Jane gently. 'And I've been watching the way you and Matt looked at each other over the weekend when you thought nobody was paying attention. It was bound to happen sooner or later.'

'Well, I, for one, wish it hadn't,' said Sian, her expression taut, as she pulled on a pair of shorts. 'It's a nuisance and a problem, and God only knows what he thinks of it all.'

'If appearances are anything to go by, he probably can't wait to get you alone, so that he can do it again!' Jane exclaimed with a laugh, but she sobered quickly enough under Sian's furious glare and asked sympathetically, 'What's the matter, love, did you like it too much?'

Her hand crept up to cover her mouth as she went a vivid, tell-tale red. She whispered, 'Oh, Jane. What am I going to do?'

'I don't know,' said her friend quietly. 'It doesn't exactly fit into your plans, does it?'

'Not in the least bit.' She bowed her head, her hair swinging forward, and she said, 'Maybe I'll go ahead and stay home for the weekend anyway.'

'Oh, Sian, but you can't! Everybody's expecting you to come along, now that your father can't come to visit!' Jane said in dismay. 'Don't you think you're over-reacting a bit?'

'I know I'm a coward. And maybe I'm being ridiculous, but—I don't know what else to do.' Then she burst out in frustration, 'Why can't we just be friends, like everybody else?'

'Darling, you might as well ask for the earth to stop revolving around the sun.' Jane reached forward and took hold of her clenched hands. 'Listen, is it such a bad thing, finding yourself attracted to a man as wonderful as Matt? So what if he changes a few of your concepts? It happens to everybody at some time in their lives. Maybe you should have a wild affair with him; at the very least it would teach you what you want in a husband.'

'I already know what I want in a husband,' she said stubbornly, her green eyes hunted. 'Faithfulness, constancy and stability.'

'And what man is going to give that to you, and still remain uninvolved?' Jane retorted. 'Even marriages of convenience have to be built on some kind of give and take, and it would certainly help if you could enjoy going to bed with your partner! Take your heart out of that safety deposit box you keep it locked in, and expose it to a few risks. It might get broken, but it'll mend. It might grow and expand to find the world a larger and better place than it was before—I don't know. But I do know one thing, Sian—if you don't learn how to break out of the shell you've built around yourself, you'll be in real danger of playing Solitaire for the rest of your life.'

Then Jane let her go to pick up the clothes in the corner, wisely giving her time to assess what she had said. Sian sank on to her bed and just sat in whirling silence, her thinking patterns all in tatters.

Had she really been cloistering herself off from the real world, under the pretext of waiting for the right man to come along? She dated, didn't she? She'd had loads of boyfriends!

And, with a sharp, chill change in perception, she looked back at them all, those earnest young men, and realised that any one of them would have given her what she'd always said she'd been looking for in a husband. None of them had been the type to stray from home, or enact the kind of subterfuge necessary for infidelity. So why hadn't she picked one and married him? What was she really looking for?

If anything, she had envisaged a relationship of equals, but when two people were real partners in strength and character, neither one was in complete control. She realised then that she could not have what she wanted without an element of trust, and she could not trust without caring. Otherwise she might as well marry somebody like Joshua, and resign herself to the sterile existence Matt had described.

Was the only other alternative to live out her life as Jane had said, playing Solitaire? Why couldn't she simply accept with good grace what fate put in her path, instead of trying to consign everything into neat, tidy little cubicles? She was a big girl now; she should be able to look after herself reasonably well. And Matt had done nothing to her that she did not want to happen.

She rubbed her eyes and sighed. Jane came up beside her and met her newly calm gaze. 'Well, what's the verdict?'

'All right,' she said. 'I can accept what you're saying. I haven't necessarily changed my thinking about a lot of things, but at least I'm willing to keep an open mind. We'll just have to wait and see.'

'And the weekend?' asked her friend with bright eyes.

'I'll come,' she said in a rush.

'That's my girl! Besides,' added Jane drily, 'there probably won't be any privacy for anything to happen even if you wanted it to.'

Sian had recovered enough of her equilibrium to smile wryly. 'Too true. Well, I've finished with reacting for one day. We'd better get back to the others.'

'Sian——' She paused with her hand on the doorknob and looked at the other woman, who continued thoughtfully, 'Maybe you'd better keep an eye on Joshua. He's been watching the way you act around Matt, and I think he might be jealous.'

'Jealous!' she exclaimed with a frown. 'What's he got to be jealous about?'

'He did want to marry you, remember?' pointed out her friend.

'Yes, but he wasn't really in love with me. It was just infatuation. He certainly took it well enough when I turned him down.'

Jane gave a careless shrug. 'Maybe I've got it wrong, but just because he can accept that you don't want to marry him, it doesn't mean that he wants to see you fall into his older brother's arms. Very dog-in-the-manger of him, I'll admit, but how like a man!'

Sian snapped, 'And who said anything about falling into Matt's arms? All I said was that I'd keep an open mind!'

Jane managed to get in a final parting shot in her ear, as she jerked open the door, 'But darling, it's already happened a few times now, hasn't it?'

That was, of course, unanswerable. Sian shook her head as they walked back into the kitchen where the three men were discussing the weekend plans. She settled into her chair again, and pretended she hadn't seen the slow, private smile on Matt's face as he looked down her long exposed legs.

The group discussed various possibilities of what to see at the theatre. Not surprisingly, Matt was well informed about many of the latest plays and musicals, and a few well-timed, pithy quotes from some of the more scathing reviews soon sent the others into fits of laughter.

'What fun it will be,' said Jane with immense satisfaction. 'I'll have to pack something civilised, I suppose—maybe my black dress, with pearls. Do you know what you're taking yet, Sian?'

She didn't know what devil came over her, but she found herself saying sweetly, as she toyed with her coffee-cup, 'I haven't made up my mind, but I have it on good authority that it should be silk, and lace—with maybe a touch of leather.'

The hazel gaze beside her lifted in quick surprise, and flared bright and hot. She raised one slim eyebrow in mocking response. Remember what I told you, Matt? Every time you turn your back, I'll be jumping out of my circle.

Sian turned her head and broke the searing contact. Her gaze wandered across the table.

She shouldn't have been surprised. Jane had warned her.

Joshua was watching them, with jealous eyes.

Sian took care on Thursday to give Joshua plenty of attention, and went to the movies with him that night, making sure throughout the evening that she acted just as warm and as friendly towards him as she ever had, without suggesting her feelings towards him had changed to that of a more romantic nature.

At first it was very awkward. Joshua arrived on the doorstep sharp and prickly around the edges, and Sian was braced for any accusing comments and questions he might make about his older brother. But Matt remained conspicuously absent from the conversation, and, during the course of the film, all the negative nuances melted away. They were both science fiction fans, and the movie thundered with dazzling special effects, a rousing adventure plot and a tongue-in-cheek humorous dialogue that had them both laughing aloud. Afterwards they went out for pizza, still chuckling and snorting like a pair of kids, and everything seemed as if it had gone back to normal.

Perhaps the jealousy she had seen in Joshua's face had been nothing more than insecurity, Sian thought as she kissed him goodnight on the cheek and ran lightly up the path to her apartment. After all, Joshua had known her first and he might have felt that their friendship was being threatened by the emergence of Matt on the scene. Matt, who represented authority and discipline, and who was that much older and self-assured and successful in his career, must be quite a formidable figure to a young man, someone to be idolised and yet resented.

In fact, Sian suspected that she wasn't actually the person Joshua was jealous of at all, but Matt might be. She had begun to notice tiny characteristics of speech and mannerisms that Joshua affected, which before she had attributed to his own personality but could now see were copies of Matthew's drawling quick-witted humour, and shrewd observances.

Joshua so wanted to be like his sophisticated, confident brother without realising that thirteen extra years of experience could not be bridged by simply acting the part. He needed to discover loss, tragedy and recovery for himself to gain wisdom, struggle through battles of his own to win true self-confidence. Some day, she was sure, he would grow to be the kind of man he admired—both he and Matt were moulded from the same thoroughbred stamp—but until then he was much as he must have been as a very young boy, watching with adoring eyes as his idol flew off to magnificent horizons he could only imagine.

Sian would have liked to test her hypothesis on Jane, but the other girl was already in bed, so she trailed through the silent apartment and turned off the lights. Everywhere she went, the tidy kitchen, the comfortable living-room, even her bedroom: all whispered with the shadow of Matt's lingering ghost. His was the type of presence that left vibrations.

She smiled wryly as she remembered Jane's suggestion to have a wild affair with him. As if an affair with him could be anything else! It would be thunder and lightning, and the occasional black howling tornado, but where in all that would be the still serenity of the eye of the storm? Where could she take shelter, bedraggled and feather-blown, from the raging elements?

Even if she accepted that her life could not be based on placidity alone and that everything worthwhile contained a certain amount of risk, she still needed the calm oasis in which to reflect and lick her wounds. She did not want to be swept off her feet to unbearable heights only to crash; she wanted a slow and graceful waltz to a classical tune, each partner's steps in harmony with the other's.

Self-knowledge was a dangerous thing. When she had not known before the breadth and depth of her desires, she had indeed been blithely content to play her intro-

spective game of Solitaire. Now her eyes had been opened
to a shimmering possibility, and it was so hauntingly
beautiful that it could only make her ache.

Uncharacteristically, she overslept the next morning
and woke around eleven feeling heavy-eyed and disgruntled. She managed to finish her chores, pack and
be ready on time, however, and dozed fitfully in the back
seat, occasionally surfacing to listen to the other three
converse. They hit the Chicago rush-hour and spent
forty-five minutes creeping along at a snail's pace, so it
was six in the evening by the time they pulled into a car
park reserved for residents and guests of a luxury block
of condominiums off fashionable Lakeshore Drive.

Everybody piled out, staring in fascination as they retrieved their luggage from the car. Lake Michigan lay
panoramic to their right, dark azure overlaid with silver
sparkles. 'Get this place!' said Steven, overacting his awe.
'Jane, my love, it's been swell, but I think I'm leaving
you for another man.'

'It is nice, isn't it?' said Joshua, with a pretence to
offhandedness that could not conceal a sense of pride.
'Matt designed the condos himself. Wait'll you see the
rest. It's got security videoscreens at the doors.'

They followed him to the door; Joshua pressed Matt's
button on the display panel, and Matt's voice came over
the intercom. 'Oh, good, you're here. Come on up.'

The lock on the door buzzed, and they entered the
cool, quiet foyer to take the lift up to his floor. When
the doors opened, Matthew was waiting in the hall, and
Sian's heart gave a great, ridiculous leap when she saw
him.

He must have gone to work, for he was still dressed
for the office, in a tan suit several shades lighter than
the bronzed outdoor hue of his complexion. Its severe

formality, combined with the carelessness of his unbuttoned collar and loosened tie, produced the strangest reaction in the pit of her stomach, a kind of sinking sensation of rabid hunger, and in her mind, uncontrollably, she imagined completing the act of pulling off his tie.

His gaze, light and brilliant, met hers briefly, then he said with a white smile, '"Welcome to my parlour," said the spider. How was your drive?'

'Fine, until we hit Chicago traffic,' said Joshua.

'Never mind, you're here now. Cold drinks are on offer to any takers, but first let's get the sleeping arrangements portioned off, so you know where to put your things. Jane and Sian, you two get the pick of my study and bedroom, Josh and Steven, you get to share the guest-room, and I'll bunk down in the living-room.'

Sian's first impression of his home was an enjoyable sense of light and space. The living-room had huge, ceiling-high windows with an unobstructed view of the shore. Sleeping in Matthew's bedroom was far too much a temptation, and before the other girl could speak up she said hastily, 'I'll take the study, thanks.'

He sent her a mocking glance, but merely said, 'Fine. Jane, your room is the next door down on the right. Sian, this is yours.'

He led her into the study and stood to one side while she looked around in curiosity and pleasure.

In front of another spacious window was an angled drawing table and high stool. The table was piled high with sheets and scrolls of papers, pens and pencils, business correspondence and a calculator. Next to one wall was a desktop computer by two tall filing cabinets, and against the third, by the door, was a short leather-bound settee where, judging by its softened and worn appearance, he obviously relaxed quite often.

There wasn't any furniture against the fourth wall, for in pride of place and covering most of the space was a huge, colourful print that she recognised as coming from the Louvre museum. 'Oh, it's lovely!' she exclaimed, stepping as close to it as she could, for on the floor underneath was a neatly made airbed.

'Thank you,' said Matt as he strolled over. 'I picked it up when I studied for a year in Paris. I'm sorry about the mess—I meant to straighten things up a bit, but didn't have the time.'

'Don't apologise, I like it.' Sian dropped her case on the foot of the temporary bed and, because she was so hypersensitive to his warm presence at her shoulder, she turned away to the drawing table and let her hand hover, eager but hesitant, over the papers. 'May I? I promise I'll be careful.'

'Help yourself.' He watched as she pored with fascination over the drawings. Painstaking and meticulous, delicately precise, and complex, they revealed a side of him that before she had only wondered at: a love of pattern, symmetry and order, and a striking flair for design. 'Some of them look rather like a rat's maze, don't they?'

'I think they're magnificent,' she breathed, rapt. 'We studied architecture in some of my design classes. Nothing in depth, mind you, but just enough to show how much training and talent goes into something like this. Look at this drawing, it's breathtaking!'

He glanced indifferently at the line-drawing of an office tower she held, and said, 'It pays the bills. That kind of project is a challenge to incorporate zoning restrictions, building codes and the specifications of the consumer, but personally I prefer designing homes for people to live in. Then the drawing seems to take on life, and breathe with all kinds of possibilities.'

She looked over her shoulder at him. 'Joshua said that you designed this block.'

He smiled crookedly into her green eyes. 'That paid the bills as well, especially as I was able to strike a deal with the developers for some cheap accommodation.'

'It's a beautiful place.'

'It's convenient for work, and certainly comfortable enough, but it's only home for now. I don't plan on living here for the rest of my life. You couldn't raise a family here, or in all conscience keep pets. You need space, and greenery, and plenty of room for them to play and explore in safety.'

Matthew held her gaze. His smile had faded away, and in its place was an intent, searching expression. She looked back at the drawing she held, struggling to hide how powerfully his words struck her. He described so perfectly the kind of quiet, spacious life that she herself desired; they could almost be picturing the same thing. In an effort to lighten the mood, she said teasingly, 'For whom to play—the kids or the pets?'

'Why not both?' he returned, strolling over to reach with a long finger to tuck a strand of hair behind her ear. The finger remained, tracing the perfect shell, while she stood rooted to the floor and shivered. 'I must confess to a secret desire to have a dog some day. Say one about, oh, knee-height, with bright, intelligent eyes and a frantic wagging tail, gentle with little children but with a great ferocious bark that would scare away any potential intruders and keep my precious wife safe when I would have to go away on a business trip. I wouldn't want to leave her too often, you see, so it would comfort me to know she was protected. You know the kind of dog.'

Her head bent forward. His fingers explored the edge of her cheek-bone, and very lightly curled against her skin. She said huskily, 'Most likely it would chew up all your shoes.'

'I'd forgive it,' he said quietly, in her ear. 'For all those other things, I'd forgive it that.'

Her hands trembled on the drawing. Carefully she turned to lay it back in its place, carefully she smoothed the immaculate edges. Then she felt a feather-light stroke across the back of her shoulders as he drew aside her hair and kissed the side of her neck. 'I'm glad you came,' he murmured against her soft, beating skin. She felt his lips part, and he stroked her pulse with a velvet tongue. 'I missed you. Did you miss me?'

Liquid waves of pleasure rippled down her back, loosening muscles and inhibitions. Her head fell to one side as he nuzzled her, as her eyelids lowered, and her breath, coming from between parted, full lips, quickened in tempo.

'Matthew,' she groaned.

'Go on,' he purred, bringing up both hands to flex those long, clever fingers around her narrow waist. 'Say it. You missed me a little bit, if only for the lack of someone to rant and rave at when you're feeling peeved.'

Her head went back against his shoulder; somehow she had come to lean on him. He spread his legs apart to support her weight, slowly running his flattened palms around the curve of her ribs and up to her breasts, and she turned her face with a sigh into his hair, raising one hand to caress his temple. She opened her mouth to confess the truth of just how much she had missed him, but just then he bit her neck with delicate savagery, and she arced and gasped, and his hands crushed her back to him convulsively.

'Matt! Where did you hide your tequila?' Joshua's shout from down the hall made her jump. For a second he continued to press her against his beating heart, and she felt the lean muscle in his jaw tighten against her cheek.

Then he laughed shortly, let go of her and whispered, 'Saved by the bell, darling?'

'You said it,' she told him huskily, 'not I.'

He seemed to freeze, but she could not look at him. Joshua shouted again, so that Matt snarled something vicious-sounding under his breath and went to answer the summons, and Sian had enough wit left to wonder just what exactly she had meant to convey by saying that.

CHAPTER SEVEN

AFTER Sian had recovered herself and checked on Jane, she made her way to the living-room where the three men appeared to be concerned with nothing more vital than the proper mixture of ingredients contained in drinks.

At her entrance, Matt looked up and said, 'We're just whipping up a batch of margaritas. Would you like one?'

She shook her head and replied with a smile, 'No, thank you. I don't drink spirits, even diluted in cocktails.'

'You're not counting calories, are you?' He cast a swift, doubtful glance down the length of her already slim body.

'No,' she said, choosing a stuffed armchair to sink into. 'I just can't take the alcohol. It puts me to sleep. A couple of glasses of wine are about my limit for the evening. I'll tell you what I would like, though—do you have any lemonade?'

'No, but I've got some fresh lemons. Would you like to make some?' She nodded, and he handed the budding concoction over to Joshua. 'Finish that up, why don't you, while I show Sian where everything is in the kitchen?'

'Sure thing. Shall I pour you a glass?'

'Yes, thanks.'

Matt led her into the compact kitchen, fetched a sharp knife and an empty pitcher, and pulled out several lemons from the vegetable container in the refrigerator, while Sian admired the butcher block inset between the stove and the sink. He laid the tart yellow fruit before her and said with a rakish grin, 'If you slice, I'll squeeze.'

She turned away, composure triumphant, and began to work. 'There you go again, always making innuendoes.'

'What did I say this time?' Sexy laughter threaded his low voice, a sultry undertone.

'You know perfectly well, and don't try playing the innocent with me. It doesn't work. You're about as innocent as a piranha!' The knife she wielded thunked satisfyingly into the butcher block, and she reached for another lemon.

'Piranhas, my love,' murmured Matthew silkily, 'only do what is in their nature to do.'

'Hi, guys,' said Jane who had wandered in. 'Matt, I love your condo. What are you talking about?'

'Fish,' said Sian. The knife thunked again. Matt leaned back against the counter and shook silently, and she shot him a sharp look. 'Matt likes piranhas.'

'Actually I prefer octopuses. All those waving tentacles,' he said, hazel eyes limpid. 'When one of those grabs a hold of something, they don't let go.'

She shuddered delicately. 'They don't even look as if they belong on this earth. They probably came from outer space.'

'Why,' asked Jane reflectively of no one in particular, 'do I get the feeling that I'm missing something here?'

'Don't worry,' Sian said soothingly, 'you're not missing a lot.'

'Oh, thanks *very* much,' drawled Matt, and she blinked wide, innocent-looking eyes at him.

'Gibberish, pure gibberish,' exclaimed the blonde in exasperation, as she turned to exit the kitchen. 'I give up on you two, I really do. You're talking in some kind of foreign language!'

'Am I, Sian?'

The quiet question came from Matthew when they were alone once more. All his lightheartedness had disappeared; he sounded brooding, grim.

She said after a moment, warily, 'What do you mean?'

'Am I speaking some kind of foreign language to you?'

The knife wavered in her hand; prudently she removed her fingers from danger, waiting until she gained more control. His strong hand clasped her wrist; her chest moved hard on a deep breath. She admitted in a shaken voice, 'I don't know.'

'Tell me.' His insistence was wearing her down, wearing her out, his hazel eyes adamant. 'Tell me when you do know.'

Her lips parted as she looked at him. Then she nodded, and he sighed, and his hand slipped away as Steven came into the kitchen with his margarita.

They settled with their drinks in the spacious living-room, talking comfortably for about a half an hour. Sian was curled on the floor, cradling a tall, cool glass of the refreshing lemonade she had made, thankful that Matt had to abandon his intimate pursuit in favour of a more general companionship.

She needed the reprieve, for she felt flustered and confused by not only his confounding behaviour, but her own complex reactions to it. Flirtation carried its own set of rules, which she knew very well, but the layers upon layers to Matt's own particular game were impossible to fully divine. Dimly she could sense the makings of a greater pattern to his intentions, in the fluidity with which he shifted from mood to mood, and, though she could not seem to glimpse his real motivations in their entirety, she was caught in the spell of fascination for how he so cleverly manipulated and anticipated her own mood swings.

The first layer was friendliness. How easy it was to relax in the warmth he could generate. Then, when he had her relaxed and open-minded, he touched her vulnerable side with confessions of his own hopes and longings and awakened in her sympathy and tenderness—all the softer emotions she had once vowed never to become entangled in when involved with a man.

And just when she was beginning to feel the fear of exposure, he danced away with a wickedness that was so irresistible to her highly developed sense of humour, she followed him along the path to bright laughter and a quick repartee interwoven with delight.

When she was angry, he slammed head on into her. When she was roused, he taunted her to a higher pitch. When she was shaken, he held her. When she goaded, he responded; when she was attracted, he lit her torch. When she was thoughtful, he challenged her.

Was this seduction? If so, it was unlike anything she had ever before experienced. Most men were so ridiculously easy to evade, for they declared their sexual intentions with about as much finesse as a trumpeting elephant. By comparison, Matthew had a manifold touch: a gossamer thread floating in the sunlit air, a rampant whirlwind rush, a quiet observation, a laughing taunt. He was straightforward and demanding, yet remained so oblique and inconclusive that every exchange of the undoubted sexual attraction quivering between them could be taken at face value alone, just another part of the flirtatious game which could lead anywhere or nowhere, nowhere at all.

She wondered, as she rested her contemplative gaze on him, smiling to herself at the mellifluous change of

expression as he listened attentively to something that
Joshua said, then responded with quick, concise logic.
How extremely clever he was, on every level. A declar-
ation of intent was a tangible thing and therefore easy
to react against, and reject. But he declared nothing,
admitted nothing, and, while she laughed, pondered,
expostulated, and tripped through every other mood he
inspired, he always kept her guessing.

Soon it was time to change for the theatre, and after
agreeing upon a system in which the girls shared the
bathroom off Matthew's bedroom, and the men shared
the other bath in the hall, they dispersed to their various
rooms.

Sian savoured the privacy of the study as she drew a
dark grey dress from her case. It was very plain, made
of an uncrushable jersey that looked good no matter
how she abused it. It moulded to the figure with length
at mid-thigh, was sleeveless and had a scooped neck and
padded shoulders. It looked severe and sexy, and almost
conventional until one caught a glimpse of the backless
plunge to the waist. She could not wear a bra with it,
of course, but then she didn't need one, for her breasts
were high, rounded and firm.

The scrapes along her back were almost healed, but
faint marks still remained. Sian covered them with a
black long-sleeved, silk turtle-neck that was so transparently sheer that every draught of air wafted through
and the lines of her arms and back were clearly visible,
yet sheathed.

The dress went over the turtle-neck, then she drew on
black silk tights, slipped her feet into the patent leather
pumps that elongated her legs, and fastened at her
narrow waist a wide black belt that came just under the
edge of the dress line at her back. Then she brushed her

sleek hair until it shone and clipped it at the nape of her neck with a plain black, extravagantly feminine bow, and, with make-up applied to emphasise her large eyes, cheekbones and a touch of red lipstick, she finally pronounced herself ready.

The evening would still be warm outside the comfortable air-conditioned coolness of the condominium, so she didn't bother with a jacket and retrieved her bag from the leather settee as she exited the study.

The men were already dressed and waiting in the living-room, formalised by their light summer-weight suits. Sian smiled to herself as the male conversation hesitated briefly at her entrance, and even Steven, who was very much in love with Jane, gave pause.

But Matthew hardly looked at her. He said briefly, 'Would you like some wine, or another glass of lemonade?'

'Wine, please, if it isn't any trouble,' she replied. It was only as she veiled the disappointment in her green eyes with dark lashes that she realised she had dressed with such care for him, and he showed no reaction at all, was even brief to the point of rudeness.

'Not at all, we'd just——'

She turned away to put her bag on the arm of a chair and exposed the graceful hour-glass curve of her cream and midnight-sheathed back to view.

If there had been a pause before, now there was dead silence. She looked around her shoulder with a slight frown. 'You'd just what?'

Joshua and Steven were staring in frank admiration. Matthew, however, had turned away and busied himself at the drinks cabinet by the wall, so his reply was muffled. 'We'd just opened a bottle while we were waiting.'

'Sian, you look exquisite,' said Joshua simply.

She forced herself to smile at him. 'Thank you.'

Matt's expression, when presented again to the group, was composed to the point of being deadpan. In high, volatile contrast were his glittering eyes, in which the lambent flecks of blue and green were very pronounced. With the thick tawny length of his hair combed under severe control and the fresh change to a grey suit much lighter than Sian's dress, he looked urbane, sophisticated and heart-stoppingly sexy.

It wasn't fair, she had time to think despairingly, as he crossed the room with a wine glass in each hand. Just the sight of him was enough to send her weak at the knees, while he revealed absolutely no reaction to her whatsoever.

As he came up to her, Jane entered the room and immediately wandered over to Steven and Joshua to coax a glass of wine for herself. Sian reached for the glass that Matt proffered, but he held on to it too long, drawing her questioning gaze up to his.

Under the cover of the shift in movement and general noise from the others, he said, softly mocking, 'I see the silk and leather. No lace?'

Piqued already, she had no thought for caution and gave free rein to her own personal devil, who murmured, 'Did I say I wasn't wearing any lace?'

His eyes shot down in lightning response to her lips and legs, for it was obvious the only other possible item of clothing she might be wearing that was not on display were her panties. 'Now, there's a concept guaranteed to send a man's temperature up a few degrees.'

She took a sip of her wine and held the liquid on her tongue to savour it, watching him over the rim as she said, 'And here I was thinking that you didn't like the cut of my cloth.'

'Like it?' His gaze sprang back up to hers, and for one unguarded moment flared hot and ravenous, while the set of his face was anything but amused. He whispered hoarsely, 'It's all I can do to keep my hands off you.'

For a suspended electric moment, they stared at each other, while Sian's world rocked under the clear, unmistakable power of his intent rigidity, the veneer of urbanity stripped clean away from the naked planes and angles of his expression.

Her eyes grew huge and her breath froze in her lungs, and, in a terrific surge of wild reaction, she didn't know if she wanted to reach blindly for the towering strength of his shoulders, or run away in terror.

Then he cocked his head at her, just a little, and smiled a tiny smile, and took up again the cloak of normality he had so impetuously cast at her feet.

Matthew said to everyone, 'We'd better leave for the theatre now. Do you want to catch a few cabs, or would you prefer walking? It's not far away, about a fifteen-minute stroll.'

The general chorus of reaction was that everyone would like to walk. Nobody seemed to notice Sian's frozen immobility or her silence; she noticed and was grateful, for she was still trying to recover from what had just happened.

She felt dizzy, concussed. The stroll to the theatre helped to clear her head somewhat. Matt led the way, while Jane had grabbed hold of Joshua's arm and was busy teasing him unmercifully. The pair bobbed and weaved erratically along the pavement, while Sian and an amused Steven brought up the rear.

She did not know how he had managed it at such short notice, but Matt had procured excellent seats for a highly

popular romantic comedy. He presented the tickets to a
woman usher who showed the group where they were
located, then he courteously stood back and let the others
file into the seats that were at the end of one row. Sian
had held back so that Jane and Steven could sit together,
and as they studied the seat numbers and compared them
with the ticket stubs Matt had handed to them, they
stopped in confusion. Joshua looked back with a frown
and said, 'There's only three here.'

'It's all right,' replied Matt, who gestured carelessly.
'The other two are over here, across the aisle. It was the
best I could get on such short notice.'

He had only voiced what Sian had thought moments
before, but she regarded him with deep suspicion, for
somehow she couldn't help but wonder if he had
somehow arranged for this to happen.

Jane was watching with bright, scarcely concealed
merriment. Sian scowled at her friend, who shrugged
expressively, then turned to cajole Joshua's sharp stare
away from his brother.

Matthew raised his eyebrows at Sian. He wore his most
guileless expression. She shook her dark, elegant head
at him, and said softly as she slid into the second seat
of the row he indicated, 'You're a very naughty man,
Matt.'

'And unrepentant, one might add,' he replied, and
put a proprietorial hand at her back. The unexpected
physical contact of his hand radiating warmth through
the sheer transparency of silk covering her skin quivered
shockwaves through her muscles, and she averted her
head sharply at his barely audible intake of breath.

'Do you always go for what you want, no matter how
unscrupulous the method?' she asked, watching him
carefully.

'That's a very subjective question,' he replied coolly as he frowned. 'And I think it depends on what your priorities are. If you want something so badly that you will do whatever you can to get it, and pay any price, some people are bound to call that unscrupulous. The key is to reach out for what you want while still maintaining your own sense of integrity. For instance, there are parts of myself that I will not sacrifice, not for love or money. Compassion, consideration, a sense of justice, and fair dealing in business are but a few. High safety standards in my work—that's another one. I'm not an idealistic man, but to me these things are paramount. If I lose them, I lose the greater part of myself, and money becomes just another dirty word, and love a meaningless commodity.'

'Faith, hope and charity?' she whispered, turning her gaze to stare unseeingly ahead of her.

'Yes,' he said with quiet simplicity, and reached out to take her hand in his.

The house lights dimmed then, and the curtains went up, and for the next few hours they laughed until their eyes teared at the light-hearted, witty play. During the interval, Joshua and Steven went to fetch ice-creams for everybody and Sian was content to relax in her seat in silence while Matt chatted with Jane, who had come over to visit them.

When the other two men had returned, and they had eaten their ice-cream and gone back to their seats to await the second half of the play, Matthew retained her hand and asked, 'Want to help me fix breakfast in the morning? I can butter the toast, but I'm not too confident about cooking eggs for five people.'

'Sure,' she agreed as she pretended her attention was fixed on the change in sets as the curtains rose again.

All of her awareness, however, was focused on the long tendoned fingers curled around hers. Then she said softly, 'Thank you again for having us. Everybody's having a wonderful time.'

His fingers tightened. He replied, 'It was all done for purely selfish reasons, I'm afraid. Will you come again?'

She turned to him, with a wide searching gaze in which the colourful stage lights flickered like tiny rainbows over the clear green depths. Her hand, in his, was very still. He watched her closely as she licked her lips and finally murmured, 'I'm not sure how easy it would be to co-ordinate the time after the others start their jobs.'

His predator's gaze held coiled patience. 'I wasn't inviting the others.'

The play rollicked on, unnoticed. She said nothing, just staring up him, but the slim fingers lying in his clasp quivered once. 'Sian,' he said then, carefully, 'why are you so afraid?'

She shook her head and would not answer.

His mouth hardened, but still he was careful. 'Will you come anyway? I'd take you dancing, and we could go to the movies, or to the park, or maybe spend an afternoon at the Art Institute. And I know when you meet them tomorrow night you'll like my friends every bit as much as I like yours.'

But underlying every picture he painted was the real question, the heart of the question. Will you come? How could she answer? That she wanted to, certainly, but that she was afraid as well, which he already knew. For every reason there was a caution, and for every caution, the dangerous, heedless desire to fling them to the winds.

'I don't know,' she said helplessly.

Her distress was obvious. He leaned over and brushed his lips against her cheek. 'There's no hurry to decide,' he murmured languidly in her ear. 'We've all the time in the world. Just promise me you'll think about it.'

And, because he had not pressed her for an answer but was instead considerate and understanding, just as he always was when he was playing the friend, she found that it was easy to meet him that far. 'A-all right.'

Matt nodded and turned his attention back to the play. Well, she thought, that was remarkably painless. She'd answered with no answer at all, which left her the freedom to vacillate as much as she wanted. Sooner or later he would want a real reply, but that was a consideration that could be put off to the foggy, indefinite future.

Besides, she found that his invitation asked more questions than it answered. All he had really done was to invite her back for another visit. He could have done the same to any one of his male friends.

Except that she wasn't one of the guys, and Matt had not invited anyone else, just her. Just her and him, together, doing things that couples do, dancing, eating out, visiting friends, walking in the park. Making love?

He hadn't asked her *that*, had he? This was the crux of the matter, the whole entire problem, the mote in her eye that was a tiny, secretive image of their bodies locked together in consummative passion.

She could always make the stipulation that if she came, she would stay in the guest-room. Then he might get offended and withdraw the invitation—how crass!—or he might agree blandly—how deflating—or he might even look at her in surprise, as if to suggest that he hadn't been considering anything else—how embarrassing. Or he might—just might—with adroit and dextrous skill set himself to changing her mind.

Which, oh dear, brought her back to the bedroom scene again.

All right, then. She would tell him no, the first chance she got. That settled things, didn't it? That put an end to the dilemma once and for all, for she didn't think that he would offer again.

And she would go home with the others on Sunday after telling Matt goodbye, thanks very much for a super time, it's been swell. She would get back to her life, go to graduate school in the autumn, just as she'd planned, and everything would revert to the normal, placid, complacent existence it had been before. No uncertainties, relatively little stress, no fast and hilarious repartee, no thrill of excitement, no burgeoning delight in her femininity, no fascination, no Matthew.

Ever.

Damn the man, and damn his confounding habit of getting under her skin. He was to blame for the quandary she found herself in—if only he had stated, when he had asked her, just what he expected from her, then she wouldn't be tying herself into knots over this, would she?

It was really very simple—how could she say yes or no when he was so busy being clever and oblique? She sat very still and quietly worked herself into an almighty fume, then started violently when the lights came up and the audience rose to their feet, clapping and whistling.

She had missed the entire second half of the play. It had vanished in a puff of sulphur, and she had so enjoyed the first part as well.

That, too, could be laid at Matt's door. When they went to a late supper at an Italian restaurant, her bad temper couldn't be contained. It spilled out of her in little biting snippets spoken through lightly clenched, smiling teeth.

The others laughed. They thought she was just being funny. But after his first thoughtful look of surprise, Matthew, who was the target of her sarcastic witticisms, started to get angry as well, and soon they were snarling and snapping at each other's heels like a pair of Yorkshire terriers.

That pleased her mightily, and so did the tight, iron-hard set to his mouth when at last the evening ended, and they strolled back to his condominium.

The heat of the day had finally dissipated, and a cool, brisk wind blew steadily off the lake. At first the chill breeze on her face was intoxicating, but then she shivered, and Matt, who had strode in dark menacing silence beside her, shrugged out of his suit jacket and held it out to her.

She refused it.

He snarled, taut and low and furious, 'Take it.'

'I don't want it!' she snapped, in pain and delight.

'I said take it!' He flung it at her violently, and it would have slid to the filthy pavement had she not clutched at the material in reflexive shock. Then, with a haughty shrug, she slung it around her shoulders and quickened her pace to join the others.

Back inside, the group made goodnight noises and dispersed to the various rooms to prepare for bed. Sian trailed Matt's jacket over the back of the couch without thanks and strode quickly for the haven of his study.

She was not quick enough. He caught up with her in the hall, and snaked one powerful hand around her upper arm.

She was jerked around to face him. She fumbled desperately for a sense of outrage at the manhandling, but instead only felt a kind of despair that glistened wetly in her hard, bright eyes. He stared at her for a long, breathless moment, then his own lowering fury seemed to disappear, leaving behind the aspect of a stern and tired man.

'You can't do it,' he said flatly.

'Do what?'

'You can't make me angry enough to withdraw my invitation.' He bent his head down to her and whispered, a bare inch from her face, 'I want you to come. Tough luck, you'll just have to learn how to handle it. So stop acting like a silly bitch, all right?'

Then he let go of her and strode back to the living-room. As she stared, he tilted back his head with a heavy sigh, yanked his tie loose, and began to shrug out of his shirt as he disappeared from sight.

She made an inarticulate, strangled sound. Oh, God, oh, God. She wanted to run to him now, throw her arms around his waist and ask for forgiveness. She knew just how silken the texture of his bare chest would be.

Instead she bolted like a rabbit for the study, shut the door behind her and leaned back, then pounded her fist against it in frustration. She had the feeling it was going to be a long and sleepless night.

CHAPTER EIGHT

SURPRISINGLY enough, however, when she had taken her
turn at the bathroom off Matt's bedroom to wash and
brush her teeth, then gone back to the study to don her
long nightshirt and slip between the covers on the soft,
cushiony airbed, she tumbled straight into a deep, heavy
sleep.

She half surfaced to a fleeting awareness occasionally
because of the unfamiliarity of her bed and sur-
roundings, and once, very early in the morning, when
the early sunrise lightened the study in spite of the closed
curtains. She blinked up at the French print that hung
over her head, then her eyes closed again and she
dreamed of Paris in the springtime.

She was strolling along the wide promenade by the
bank of the Seine river when it started to rain, soft and
warm against her upturned cheeks. A group of smiling
Japanese tourists offered her an umbrella, but she shook
her head. She liked the gentle rain; it soothed and caressed her skin with long, sensitive fingers and whispered
the satiny words, Wake up, darling. Won't you wake
up?

She sighed and turned on to her side, and opened her
eyes as she came off the airbed and lay like a burrowing
animal underneath the untidy shelter of her covers.

Matt knelt over her, cupping her face with his hands.
Her sleepy, bemused gaze travelled all over him. He was
shirtless and shoeless, clad only in a pair of faded jeans,

135

and he smelled soapy clean, warmly male, his damp, tawny hair combed back from a freshly shaved face.

'Wake up, darling,' he whispered, stroking her softened lips with the ball of his thumb.

'Hi,' she murmured, still half asleep and blissfully, luxuriously languid. Surprised by pleasure, without the memory of the need for defence or barriers or inhibiting insecurities, her lovely green eyes smiled up at him.

Something shook over his face, a kind of wonderment, and with a sigh that sounded like surrender he bent down and kissed her vulnerable mouth. With an action that seemed as natural as breathing, she reached up to stroke her fingers through his cool, damp hair to the back of his head, while her heavy eyelids fluttered shut.

He shifted under her caress, a sensuous movement of inarticulate delight, while his lips wandered, mobile and explorative, over the contours of hers. An indolent heat washed through her reclining body, which stretched and turned in instinctive response. His hands moved from her face to slide along the slender stalk of her neck, over the light cotton material of her nightshirt, down her exposed torso.

To touch her was to know her: all the delicate beating hollows of sensitivity, the grace in her curved ribcage, the soft firm mounds of her breasts which tingled with a new and exciting fire as he brushed against them.

She was drowning in a wellspring of sheer desire, wandering a vast uncharted territory where the shape and strength of his naked, muscled shoulders were both guide and anchor. Her mouth opened like an amazed flower; he groaned at the gift, and took it with breathless care, searching deep in the intimate crevices for further paths of subterranean delight, pushing her head back against the carpet.

Her hands at his shoulders twisted and shook, and slipped with an intensified sensory shock down the tensile expanse of his powerful back, and collapsed his body into a downward arc that brought his full weight on to her.

He was heavy, such a big, strong man, but she was so meltingly boneless that the contact only heightened the whirling pleasure, erecting through the thin T-shirt her nipples that were crushed against his chest, deepening the empty ache between her legs. His mouth quickened over hers, taut and slanted with fierce demand, drawing, calling upon her, building her desire to a heat that dampened the tendrils of hair at her temples and shook her breathing with unfulfilled stress.

She moaned with soft incomprehension, for the empty ache was becoming an agony, and in instant passionate response he thrust one heavy knee between her legs, his entire length throbbing hard and aggressive, at breast and hip and the soft, innocent arc of her pelvis.

The bedcovers were an infuriating barrier. She couldn't stand it; rational thought in the heart of this mating was an impossibility. She twisted under him in urgent frustration, and the grip of his hand over her breast tightened painfully... and he arced back his head with a tortured gasp, breaking the melded contact with her mouth, and it was such a brutal withdrawal, so like the last time, that her face twisted in a harsh sob of protest.

'God!' The exclamation tore out of him raggedly, and he trembled from head to toe. 'Sian, my God, help me stop.'

'I don't want to.' The words dragged out of her, nearly incoherent, and he gripped her head with both hands.

'Neither do I.' His whisper was a groan. 'But not here, not now—with the others in the apartment——'

Her eyes flared open, wild and brilliant with a harsh return to sanity, and she groaned deeply, 'Oh, no.'

'Darling, I'm so sorry,' he breathed, and stroked the tight, distressed line of her cheek. 'I didn't mean for it to happen like this, to get so out of hand——'

It was such torment, to feel and see and want him so badly that it brought tears to her eyes, and her face clenched as she turned away sharply from him and gritted, 'Get out.'

'I can't,' said Matthew harshly. 'Not until I know you're all right.'

'Yes, yes, I am, just *please*—go away and give me a few minutes to pull myself together!' Her voice broke on the last word, and for a suspended instant she felt his thoughts as surely as she felt his thudding heartbeat against hers: his wordless, almost uncontrollable desire to give her comfort which would be the last, fatal straw, for she could not deny it, no more than she could deny him anything else he wished for in that moment.

Then he pulled away from her, in a silence that screamed reluctance, and said quietly, tightly, 'I'll be in the kitchen.'

Go. Go. She wrapped her arms around herself, huddling underneath her covers until the door shut behind him. Then she groaned, a long, animal sound, and shivered as though she had a high fever.

The aftermath of such a fierce, unconsummated desire was something she didn't know how to cope with. She didn't have the tools; her only knowledge of sex was that of a textbook kind. She knew all about the facts of sexual frustration and fulfilment, but she had never experienced them for herself, and her body was an untapped vessel.

She had never before considered herself to be a prude. She had kissed, and indulged in some petting with a few of her dates, but it had always been a light, mild sort of pleasure that did not stir the heart and mind to uncontrollable recklessness. In consequence, she had found it almost too ridiculously easy to refrain from going to bed with anyone, and had gradually come to assume that she would wait until she could give her virginity to her husband. It had seemed, in the cold-blooded light of day, to be one more asset she could bring to a marriage, especially in today's society when the indulgence of casual sex carried its own dangers.

But Matthew called upon something ingrained and atavistic in her. Effortlessly they seemed to strike right at the heart of each other's archetypal instinct.

Him. Making her crazy, infuriating her, pushing her, pursuing her, driving her where he wanted her to go. Sian's tousled head turned restlessly on her pillow. She was tired of running, tired of denying, tired of reasons and fears. She was tired of being pushed too far without culmination. What to do about it? Pare to the essence in the hunt for resolution, damn the consequences, and shove him back.

She smiled slowly, green eyes glowing, and for the first time since meeting Matthew felt at peace.

Decision was a wanton lady.

After a time, she stirred herself to prosaic action, tidied and made her bed, searched through her luggage for the small cloth bag that held her cleansing cream and toothbrush. When she slipped down the hall to the bathroom, it was empty, so she entered, locked the door behind her and stood for several minutes under a stinging, cool shower spray. It soothed her hot, flushed body and cleared her mind, and, after shampooing and soaping all over, she went back to the study and pulled on a black vest top and a loose, comfortable pair of sky-blue bermuda shorts.

She'd had time to remember why Matt had come to wake her up, and went to the kitchen in search of him. The scent of fresh coffee filled the air as she rounded the corner.

Matt had donned a white T-shirt and was busy at the butcher block counter, halving grapefruit. Though she had moved silently, his tawny head lifted and he turned to the doorway.

His expression was very serious, the hazel eyes overshadowed in a way she had never seen before. They moved over her pale, carved face and steady gaze, and, with a slight shake of his head, he sighed and said, 'Sian, I am sorry.'

The deep self-accusation in his voice cut her to the quick, so she cut back, with verbal stiletto. 'Ooh,' she cooed sweetly, 'regrets so soon? That doesn't augur well for any future visits, does it, darling?'

His head reared back. He stared at her narrowly. 'Are you all right?'

She gave him a tight, sour smile and strolled into the room. 'I won't pretend that I'm not—disturbed.'

He laid down his knife and took a step forward, and stopped dead when she jerked back in instant reaction. 'Do you know,' he said then, sounding so very odd, 'that I wouldn't want to hurt you for anything?'

'What's the matter, Matthew,' she mocked, cocking her head to one side, 'are you afraid I'll break? Going to handle me with kid gloves? It's a trifle late for that, don't you think?'

He averted his face sharply, nostrils flared, and admitted harshly, 'I guess I deserved that.'

Her eyes gleamed with the liqueur of excitement. Push him again. 'Humility, no less,' she drawled, and he jerked towards the counter to hold on to the edge with both hands. 'This is getting fun. If you lie on the floor, I can kick you some more.'

'For God's sake!' he growled, lowering his head as if in deep labour. His knuckles were white. 'Why don't I just point out my jugular so you can lunge for that?'

She took a step closer, hackles raised to the intoxicating sense of danger. How far was his limit? 'OK by me,' she said insolently, watching with immense satisfaction his ivory jaw, his goaded eyes. 'Since you feel so obliging.'

Just the tiny neat inclination of his head gave the impression that he rounded on her like a snarling animal at bay. Nearly there now. 'Watch what you say, lady,' he growled softly. 'You were a willing participant in that little scene.'

Her eyebrows raised. 'You mean you were in a state to actually notice?'

He hung his head, bared his strong clenched teeth. He looked drugged. 'Just what the hell do you want from me?'

Ah, there was the edge. Time to push him over. She shot forward, slapped a hand on the counter beside his and snapped, 'I wondered when you'd get around to asking me that!'

'Back off,' he whispered, hazel eyes wide.

'I want to fight,' she told him throatily, and pushed her face into his; ah, but she'd learned from an expert.

He couldn't help but read the evidence in front of him: the ruthless glitter of her eyes, the dark colour along her cheek-bones, the angle of her wand-slim neck that was both taunt and offering. She smiled sexily, and enunciated in intimate provocation, 'And then I want a *good—hard—rousing——*'

He gasped, and whirled, and suddenly they were together, holding each other in a tight, bruising hug. Her head fell back as she smirked at him. He shook her, his eyes ablaze, and she reached up to cover those hazel orbs with one hand that slipped, and stroked his darkened cheek, and his mouth fell ravening on to hers. He thrust his tongue, and she suckled it, and he crushed her aching breasts with shaking hands, and she writhed against him in fierce ecstasy.

Then they heard doors open and close, the distant sound of the shower starting in the hall bathroom.

They leaped apart as if scalded, and ended up at opposite ends of the kitchen. She stared at his back as he presented it to her. He gripped his head with both hands and hissed, 'Did I ever say I liked your friends? I hate them, so passionately——'

The sound of Jane's sleepy voice came down the hall. '—don't know what time it is. Somebody's awake, though. I can smell the coffee.'

By the time Jane emerged on the scene, Matt was back at the cutting board, while she was busy pulling margarine, bacon and a carton of eggs from the refrigerator. Such a bland and domestic scene, but the margarine fell on the floor from her nerveless fingers, and Matt, she noticed, did not cut any more grapefruit, but spun one half in repeated circles.

'Good morning, sleepyhead,' he said to Jane without looking at her. He almost sounded normal.

Jane blinked like an owl and yawned noisily. 'God, you both look disgustingly alert. How long have you been up?'

'Forever,' muttered Matthew in despair.

Sian walked drunkenly to the stove, her arms full. 'Not long,' she said to her friend. 'I just took a shower. Want an egg?'

'Mmm, please. I'm going to jump in Matt's shower first, if his water-heater will hold up with both going.'

He growled, 'It'll stay hot.' Sian was laughing like a crazy woman, and he shot her a speaking glare.

'I'll bring you in a cup of coffee, then I'll cook your breakfast,' she offered, wiping damp hands on a towel and reaching for the cups in the cupboard.

'Isn't she wonderful?' murmured Jane affectionately to Matt. 'I just love her to bits.'

His knife clattered as he threw it into the sink. 'Oh, she's peachy, all right.'

She slammed the cupboard shut with a resounding bang, and this time he laughed. With a pained wince Jane left the noisy pair.

Soon Steven and Joshua were lured into the kitchen by the aromatic smell of bacon sizzling under the grill, and buttery eggs frying, and Sian was kept busy cooking for everyone for the next half-hour or so, until Jane claimed the skillet and made her sit down to eat.

Jane and Sian decided to go shopping that morning, which none of the men seemed too keen to go along with, so they arranged to meet for lunch. The group parted in the street; Sian watched as Matt strolled away with Joshua and Steven.

In the strong sunlight, he looked casual and relaxed. Joshua turned to say something to him, at which he shrugged. Then before they disappeared from sight around the nearby corner, he stared back at the girls, shading his gaze with one hand.

She turned quickly back to Jane, who had asked her a question. 'That's fine with me,' she said, having no idea what it was she had agreed to.

'Then Marshall Fields it is,' said the blonde with satisfaction. 'After all, they're such a big department store, they'll have everything under one roof, and we only have a couple of hours before we meet the others.'

They saw an empty taxi and hailed it. It promptly slewed across the lanes, to the annoyance of the other drivers, and whisked them away. Then, at the store, they browsed through sportswear, lingerie, and the perfume and accessories counters.

Sian trailed along behind Jane like a ghost, stopping when the other girl stopped. After she had stood, staring fixedly at a rack of garments for several minutes, Jane noticed her preoccupation and came up to her.

'You don't really want to buy that, do you?'

At the doubtful question said softly into her ear, Sian started and looked about. She was at the edge of the maternity section of clothing, and the dresses she'd been gazing at were huge tent-like things designed more for comfort than high fashion.

'God, no!' she exclaimed violently and swung away. 'I was just thinking, that's all.'

'Oh, thinking, were you?' replied Jane wisely. 'I'm relieved. For a moment there, I thought you might be in love.'

'With those?' She looked comically horrified. Jane merely raised her eyebrows, and she hunched one defensive shoulder and sidled over to a display of scarves, running the shimmering, patterned material through her fingers. The silence was eloquent, and too prolonged.

To break it, she said belligerently, 'Well, what if I am in love?'

'With the maternity dresses?' Jane assumed astonishment. Sian's breath whistled inwards, a high, beleaguered whine, and the blonde relented. 'Honey, I'm sorry. I won't tease any more.'

She lifted her chin. 'Doesn't matter. I'm not, anyway. In love, I mean.'

'Of course you're not,' Jane soothed.

Her fingers rubbed on the scarf, back and forth, back and forth. 'After all, I've only known him a week.'

'Not at all a reasonable time schedule for falling in love,' her friend agreed. 'And he did save your life.'

She was outraged and befuddled. 'What the hell does that have to do with anything?'

'Oh...' the blonde girl waved vaguely '...saviour infatuation, or something.'

'I happen to think that what Matt did that day said a lot about the man!' Sian bristled, glaring at her friend. 'He acted in a selfless and courageous manner, putting the boy's and my safety before his own! He was gentle, and considerate, and competent, and attentive and—and—oh, God.'

'Yes, love?'

Sian dragged the scarf to her face and hid in it. The rack on which the scarf was hooked clattered to the counter, and attracted the attention of a sales clerk, who hurried over. 'I am in love with him, aren't I?' she whispered.

Jane said gently, 'Yes, love.'

'That makes it sound so simple,' she said to the scarf.

'It sounds simple enough, but even simple things aren't always the easy ones.' She lifted her head, and Jane pried her fingers from the scarf to hand it back to the disapproving clerk. The clerk scowled at Sian, who smiled back at her bewilderedly.

Jane guided her through the department store and out to the street. It was nearly one o'clock, so they went to meet the others in a fashionable brasserie that had high French windows along the front which opened to a wide expanse of pavement where tables and chairs were set in a continental style. The men were already relaxing outside with cold drinks.

Sian could feel Matt's thoughtful, brooding gaze on her but, in an agony of uncertainty, she couldn't bring herself to look at him. She chose a seat well away from his indolently outstretched length.

Throughout the rest of the sunny afternoon, she avoided any direct contact with him, gravitating instead towards the uncomplicated companionship of the others as the group went to the zoo and walked along the various enclosures. She knew she was behaving in a manner inconsistent with that morning, but she couldn't help herself; she felt suspended in a single moment of time, a nocturnal animal frozen in the glaring headlights of a car, not knowing which way to escape, just waiting, fatalistically, for the impending collision.

He didn't chase her. Indeed, he strolled along with every appearance of ease, the strong sunshine lightening his windswept tawny hair with strands of light gold, his eyes vivid against the tanned darkness of his handsome features. He carried on a light, effortless flirtation with Jane, who laughed and gave as good as she got, while Sian, for the first and only time in her life, burned with miserable jealousy for the attention he gave her friend.

They went back to his condominium at six in the evening, to get ready for the party. People were due to start arriving at eight, so everyone pitched in to prepare the food before changing clothes. There was a plentiful supply of food: cheese, crackers, cold chicken, beef and pâté, potato chips, a ham and broccoli quiche already ready for the oven, pickles and olives. All that needed to be done was to arrange everything on the dining-table at the end of the large living-room area, and to shift the couch and chairs so that there was a large open space for dancing.

Sian changed into a pale lemon sleeveless top with a matching ankle-length, gauzy skirt that flowed gracefully with the movements of her long legs. With a wide red belt, and chunky red jewellery that was in striking contrast to her pale skin, her shining black hair flowing unconfined, she looked slim and colourful, and very feminine.

Her face showed no hint of her turmoil, nor the inner wince she felt when Joshua put some bouncy music on the excellent stereo and it jangled a loud intrusion on her sensitised nerves. To anyone watching she appeared to be enjoying herself in a quiet, good-natured fashion, and, when the guests began to arrive and the condominium filled to overflowing, she found to her surprise that somewhere she had stopped acting the part and actually was having a good time.

She did like Matt's wide, gregarious circle of friends. Their careers, ages and lifestyles differed hugely; about the only thing they seemed to have in common was a universal high opinion of their host, who was immensely popular with both sexes.

Of course the advantage in having a host to such an occasion was that he was sure to invite all his male friends. Sian noticed in amusement that Jane had bright shining eyes like a child set loose in a candy shop, and that Steven hovered very close to her with his jaw set.

She found herself in great demand as a dancing partner, and had just consented with a laugh to yet another dance with a very funny, attractive colleague of Matt's when he appeared at her shoulder and told the other man bluntly, 'Buzz off, Rick. Sian's dancing this one with me.'

She cocked an ironical eyebrow as his friend took the interjection philosophically. 'I might have known you'd have your eye on the most beautiful woman in the room.'

He put his arm around her shoulders. 'That's right, but if you're quick, the little blonde in the corner is good company. She's also Sian's best friend, so mind your manners, hear?'

'Yes, Papa Matt,' said Rick with a grin as he turned to locate Jane, who was talking to Steven. His eyes lit up appreciatively. 'Don't I always?'

'I'm not sure I approve of you setting Jane up like that,' remarked Sian, as she watched Rick thread his way through the people to her friend.

'Rick's OK,' said Matt with a sidelong glance and a smile. 'He's a bit of a Casanova, but great fun as light relief, and he's not intimidated by an intelligent woman. Besides, it won't do Steven any harm to feel the burn of a little competition.'

They bore witness to the first encounter. Rick reached the couple and said something, and Steven scowled but Jane turned her melting gaze up to the other man and said something in reply that creased Rick's face with surprise and delight.

Matt's arm tightened around Sian's shoulders as he said quietly, 'Now, what about that dance?'

'I haven't heard you ask me yet,' she replied coolly, still disgruntled at how he had arrogantly assumed that she was his for the taking.

But wasn't she? Oh, wasn't she?

He turned around to face her, and cupped the soft upper flesh of her arms with a warmth of grip that sent a reactive shiver down her spine, and, with a sombre look in his keen, intent eyes, he said grimly, 'That's because, after avoiding me all day, I was afraid you'd say no.'

She scowled and said to his chest, 'Don't be silly, I haven't been avoiding you.'

'Then you won't object to a dance, will you?' He opened his fingers and slid the flat of his hands with slow, infinitely patient sensuality around to the small of her back and pulled her to him.

The entire day might never have happened. In a blinding flash, she was back in the molten, mind-destroying build-up of eroticism from that morning, and her slender body bowed to his hard length like a vulnerable reed before a storm. She had to put her arms around his waist; he was the only port of stability in the increasingly violent tremors that racked through her, breaking down her fragile poise.

He made some kind of sound, a taut, incoherent exclamation, and his head lowered to rest against the top of hers as he tightened his hold so that she thought he would break her spine. Then in a quick, snaking movement that whirled her into breathless shock, he pulled them both out of the crowded room and down the hall.

Sian was distressingly close to tears. She could no more comprehend the reason for it than she could take into her numb mind the direction in which they were going. Her legs functioned automatically to the demand of his long, swift stride while his arm was an unbreakable band of steel around her waist, and the profile of his face, when she glanced up, was fixed and rigid.

The study was empty and dark. He did not bother with shutting the half-closed door or turning on the light, but instead went straight to the end of the settee where he turned to sit and grip the edges of it, regarding her with a terrible, helpless hunger.

He had let her go upon entering the room. She stood, half in shadow with the hall light crowning the black sleek fall of her hair with a dusky aureole of coppery gold. Frightened obscurely, she folded her arms across her chest and regarded him in equal measures of apprehension and belligerence.

'Sian,' he said. He made her name into a soft caress of sound and air, and then again, with a siren's lure of simplicity, 'Sian.'

She took a faltering step towards him, and his hands tightened on the settee until even she could see in the shadows how the cords in his wrists stood out in silvery relief.

'Tell me,' she whispered, needing it so badly she shook. 'For God's sake, just tell me.'

The words came out of him, dragged into existence with hard effort at control. 'I am trying, good God, I'm trying to be patient, but it's a little difficult when I want you so badly I can hardly see straight.'

His naked bluntness sizzled down her body with as much galvanising power as if he had physically touched her, and she bit into the heel of her hand with an audible catch of her breath.

'I want you,' he said slowly, watching her. 'I want to be inside you. You drive me insane, and I want to make you as crazy, I want to hear you cry out with it. Just a smile from you can make me weak at the knees with pleasure. The touch of your skin is finer than any silk, the scent of your hair goes to my head like wine, and the new-washed colour of your eyes when you wake up in the morning is a sea wide enough to drown my senses.'

Somehow he had lost the febrile tension from a moment ago, and lounged back with lazy grace. Her eyes peering over her hand were massive, and she groaned, half in terror, 'Oh, you could talk the sun out of the sky, you could.'

'I want to watch your face when you climax,' purred gentle temptation. 'Reach out, Sian. Kiss me, please, with your soft and sweet lips. Touch me, stroke me, do what you like with me. I do bite, but only if you want me to. Come to me, and pleasure yourself. It's been forever since this morning, and I'm dying for it.'

'And if I do, where does that leave us?' she challenged, his seductive invitation playing havoc with her feverish imagination.

'Darling, how should I know? I'm no prophet. The future will be whatever it will be.' He cocked his head and suggested throatily, 'Would one more kiss from you make us enemies or lovers?'

She could no more resist him than she could resist herself. She took another step forward, and another. He shifted to part his long outstretched legs further, allowing her to come up between them, and his head fell back as he watched her, and the open eager desire in his eyes was the last thing she saw as she started to lower her head to his, and the pervasive sweetness of the surrender was far greater than anything he had promised her before, burnished as new as the first time, yet leavened with voluptuous memory.

'What about—just good friends?' she whispered, leaning the heated flow of her body against his inner thighs.

'Oh, yes,' he murmured, tilting his face, 'whatever happened to them?'

Her lips came down and touched his in a light, flower-petal caress, and the blissful agony of his self-restraint transmitted itself in the heightened stress of his breathing She could feel his wide chest labour deliciously as she brought her hands to rest on the front of his shirt, running them up the covered muscle to the column of his neck, which beat a rapid tattoo against the tips of her fingers.

Then, when she lifted her head, he twisted sharply and said, with quick and urgent pleading, 'No, don't——'

'Don't what?' she murmured, lost in the strains of the languid dance.

'Don't go,' he groaned, and reached with one hand to rake her head back down and plunge into her mouth.

The roaring bonfire had them writhing together in an ascendant blaze that fused mouth to mouth, heart to racing heart, and her arms twined around his neck, and his hold was an inescapable bond around her body.

She fell victim to the loss of his seductive control, as his fingers clenched into her hair, and he broke from the kiss to run his hot, open, trembling lips along the line of her cheekbone to the sacrificial stalk of her neck. Mindlessly she raked her fingernails along the width of his back, and his harsh resultant gasp melted her like wax.

They were both so engrossed in each other that neither heard the quick, light footsteps over the loud music blaring from the living-room, or Joshua calling out, 'Matt? Sian?'

The light in the study came on, and shattered the silver-shadowed intimacy into incandescent shards.

Matt's head reared back. She jerked in surprise and would have pulled out of his arms, except his hand at the back of her head, around her waist, held her stationary. All she could do was stare into the glittering pools of his eyes as he looked beyond her to his younger brother.

Whatever he saw in the heavy, dead silence behind her made his face settle into hard stern lines. He said to Joshua coolly, 'I'll be out in a minute.'

The other man said nothing, but the sharp report of the door slamming spoke volumes, and Matt looked down at her with a frown. Her expression had filled with distress, her green eyes clouded with concern. She whispered, 'God, I—just didn't think. Maybe I'd better go talk to him.'

'No,' he said with a sharp sigh, 'I'll do it. Are you all right?'

'That's the second time today you've asked me that,' she murmured, and his hold tightened.

'I thought the first time was bad enough, but if you're now feeling anything like I am, you've just been pole-axed.' He stared at her grimly. 'This doesn't change you and me. If you think it does, to hell with talking to Joshua, I'm going to stay right here and kiss you until you come to your senses.'

And what are we?' she asked him, with a wistful smile. 'Enemies, lovers, or just good friends?'

He stared at her. 'Don't go back to South Bend tomorrow. Stay here with me.'

Her eyes fell to the opening of his white shirt, and she muttered, 'Oh Matthew, I—I don't know.'

'Why not?' he asked. His hard hands were branding marks on her. 'You're not going back to a summer job. Why couldn't you stay?'

'But for how long?'

He shrugged, a careless movement that belied the cool, deep shadow of thought moving at the back of his hazel eyes. 'A few days, a week, a month. Hell, who knows, you might end up staying the whole summer and liking it.'

Her face twisted. 'My things are in South Bend—my friends, clothes, school, plans.'

He was harsh. 'All I know is that if you leave now, you'll spend all your spare time making up reasons not to come back, and erecting your barriers, and Chicago is too far away for me to be popping back every weekend just to try to change your mind.'

'But,' she argued, fiddling with the top fastened button, 'maybe we need time to think.'

'See what I mean?' he replied drily. 'There goes another barrier, and you're not even out of my arms yet. We don't need more time alone, we need it together, to explore one another in depth, to find out what we enjoy about each other, and what we disapprove of, to make love in the long warm evenings, and the dark cool of early morning.'

Her fingernail jerked and the button slipped free, and at the exposure of yet more of the hair-sprinkled skin of his chest, she recalled the pressure and excitement of his hard body pinning her to the floor. Why was she hesitating? It was what she wanted. She leaned her forehead against him.

'Please,' she whispered. 'Ask me in the morning. Don't ask me now.'

He sighed into her hair and his arms loosened. 'All right. Tell me tomorrow. In the mean time, I'd better go find Joshua and have a talk with him. Do you want to come out with me?'

She shook her head and said, muffled, 'I'll be out in a few minutes.'

He dropped a kiss on to the top of her forehead and straightened from the settee. Already he was absent-minded, thinking ahead to other things. 'Fine. Just don't talk yourself out of something that would be good for the both of us.'

But what about the long run, Matt? she asked, but silently, as he left and shut the door behind him. Never mind about tomorrow, or the day after, or the week after that. What about a year from now? Who's to say what would be good for us then? What about the rest of our lives?

CHAPTER NINE

BOTH Matthew and Joshua were conspicuously absent when Sian finally mustered up the energy to leave the study. She had brushed her hair and touched up her make-up, so that the only evidence of what had happened lingered in the over-bright glitter of her eyes and the hectic flush staining the high curves of her cheekbones.

At first glance the party still seemed to be in full swing, but, with used plates stacked in the kitchen sink, glasses littering the counter and most of the people sitting and talking in the living-room instead of dancing, it looked as though it might wind to a close very soon.

She checked her wrist-watch and found to her shock that it was already well past midnight. Jane came up and whispered in her ear, 'Lordy, where have you been? You missed the fireworks. Joshua just came storming into the room, looking like a thunder-cloud, and Matt came in soon after, stern and hard and cold as you please, and he took Josh into the bedroom. They're in there now and it's ominously quiet, don't you think?'

She pressed one hand against her hot cheek and closed her eyes, confessing shakily, 'I didn't entirely miss the drama. Matt and I were in the study, and Joshua came in and found us together.'

Jane's eyes were very wide. 'What were you doing?'

'Well, we weren't exactly discussing the weather!' she snapped in an explosive release of tension, though she immediately regretted it. 'Look, I'm sorry. I'm just strung out.'

'No wonder.' Her friend studied her closely and with a great deal of sympathy. 'Don't blame yourself Sian. None of this is your fault. You never encouraged Joshua. Whatever he built up out of your relationship with him was entirely in his own head, so try not to worry. Matt will sort him out, you'll see.'

'I hope so,' she said, but there was a wild, hunted look in her eyes. Immediately Jane put one arm around her shoulders and led her into the relative privacy of the kitchen, where she sank against the counter.

'Tell me,' urged Jane in a gentle voice.

Sian stared blankly at her feet. 'Matt's asked me to stay tomorrow instead of going back to South Bend with the rest of you.'

'Is that all?'

'Is that all?' she echoed incredulously, her green eyes flashing up to her friend's compassionate, but calm expression. 'Jane, the very thought terrifies me! I love him so much it hurts, and I have no idea what his intentions are, or how long it might last.'

'Then you must stay,' Jane said simply, reaching out to grasp her hands. 'And love him for as long as you can.'

Her head shook from side to side, and her eyes filled with pools of salted wetness that streaked *diamanté* paths down her marble cheeks. How could she explain this crisis of uncertainty? In just a week she had travelled too far from what had been a corner-stone of belief in her life, and to reach out for what she wanted now would be to deny every best judgement she had always believed in. She wasn't a gambler like her father. She was just a young woman who was frightened to find that the understanding she had built her hopes and dreams on had turned to shifting sand underneath her feet.

'Don't you see?' she said, almost begging. 'It's too soon. It happened too quickly. I don't even know what he feels for me, beyond the physical attraction. Maybe someone else might have the strength of mind to take such a risk, but I don't know if I can.'

'Then come home,' said Jane and squeezed her cold hands. Then she added with quiet, relentless wisdom, 'But if you do, you must be prepared to let Matt go. Because some day, some time, he will find a woman who can, for she will recognise how much courage it took for him to risk opening up his heart and his life to her.'

Every strong emotion inside her rose up in nauseous rebellion at the thought of Matthew living with, and loving, another woman, and she flinched back as if she'd been slapped in the face. Through a roaring in her ears, she heard her friend ask, 'Does the consideration of that, if nothing else, give you an answer?'

She whispered through bloodless lips, 'Yes, I rather think it does. I'll stay, if he'll still have me.'

'Oh, Sian.' Jane stepped close and hugged her tight. 'I couldn't wish for you to find a better man, but I am going to miss you!'

She put her arms around the other girl and laid her head on Jane's shoulder, exclaiming, 'What's this? I might only be gone a few days.'

'Then again, you might not,' said Jane, who stepped back and wiped her eyes. 'Which is only how it should be.'

Just imagining how it would be to wave goodbye to the others, then find herself alone with Matt at last with all the private future stretched before them, was enough to send her blood-pressure soaring. She was beside herself with excitement, consumed with dread. Would they be able to fill the empty space with light and laughter? Or would all her new emotions collapse under the weight of it? Would she discover after the first heated rush that she was merely caught in the illusory spell of infatuation? And he—how would he feel? Would he regret his invitation after a few brief days, or might he also fall in love with her?

She knew then that she was doing the right thing, for all the questions had assumed an imperative place in her mind, and there would be no rest, no peace, no hope for her until they were answered.

When the two men emerged from Matt's bedroom at last, there was no chance to find out how things stood between them, for Matt's attention was claimed by the departure of his guests, and Joshua was remarkably silent and subdued, and refused to meet her questioning gaze.

She schooled herself to patience as best she could, but her concern was growing into a deep, unsettled unease, for the shape of Matt's mouth was a straight white line, and his eyes when they met hers briefly were cold with a kind of bitten-back fury that was all the more disturbing for the severe control he exerted over it.

The spectre of the scathing stranger she had confronted just a week ago rose in her mind. With an inward shudder, she banished the terrible ghost to the past where it belonged, for neither of them were really the people who had enacted that scene. She had worn, albeit unknowingly, the misshapen cloak of someone else's caricature of her personality, and Matt had fleshed out since that time to become a real, full-blooded person with strengths and vulnerabilities, and a deep-bedded core of compassionate wisdom that made him so extraordinary.

She marked time, going into the master bathroom to wash her face and brush her teeth, denying for as long as possible the need to go to Matt and discover what had caused that taut set of his mouth, or scored the deep lines on either side of it. She wanted to hug him, and stroke his tawny hair, and tell him that she was willing to stay for as long as they both wished it.

She drew on her light wrap of summer cotton that came to mid-thigh, and belted it at her slim waist as she walked back through the bedroom, wished Jane good-night, and went to the study.

The light was on. Matt sat on the high stool facing the drawing-table, his back to the doorway. His hair looked ruffled, as if he had run his hands repeatedly through it, and she ached to smooth it back from his forehead.

She smiled involuntarily and stepped inside the room. 'Hello there,' she said. 'I was just going to look for you.'

His head turned to one side. 'Funny,' he said flatly. 'I came in here looking for you, but I half expected you to have made other sleeping arrangements.'

The short, clipped voice, and the glimpse of the hard line of his jaw made her hesitate. Why wouldn't he turn around? If he only smiled at her, she would run to him with open arms, but this—she didn't know how to react to.

'I don't understand,' she said quietly.

'You're always running away,' said Matthew, with a thin slicing edge of sarcasm. 'You did it from the start. Even the first time we met, when I gave you hell, you ran away.'

A frown creased her brow. 'But I'm not running now— you've got it all wrong. I told Jane that I wasn't going back to South Bend with them.'

'You're going to try to convince me that you want to stay?' he asked harshly. 'That's taking it a bit far, even for you, isn't it?'

She didn't know what was going on, but her heart thudded hard in apprehension, and she licked suddenly dry lips. 'Matt, look at me.'

He swivelled around and thrust off the stool, in a stunning upsurge of movement, and the deep rage in his face was so far beyond what she had feared that she fell back a step and stared, one hand creeping up to cover the frantic beating at the base of her throat.

He asked fiercely, his lips drawn back, 'And just when was it you were planning on telling me that you'd become engaged to Joshua—early in the morning, just before you left? Were you saving it for pillow talk? Damn you for a lying bitch!'

The bottom of her world seemed to drop away at the severity of his accusation, and she swayed on her feet. God, oh God, how could she have forgotten that little piece of mischief she and Joshua had cooked up between them? She whispered on a shuddering breath, 'He told you?'

Matt's eyes had widened at her stricken expression, and for a moment his own cracked to reveal the aspect of a man floundering deep in grief, then his face hardened into razor-edge angles.

'So,' he said with the staccato force of a bullet. 'It was true. I'd wondered at first. Joshua can act like a petulant brat when he doesn't get his own way, and somehow I couldn't quite believe it of you. There was no way that you could be the coolly calculating woman Joshua had made you out to be. You seemed so vulnerable, and innocent despite that veneer of poise you wore, that I had completely revised my first opinion of you. I didn't even listen when you warned me that you'd get me somehow in the end. Well, congratulations, sweetheart! You took me in hook, line and sinker, and I hope the satisfaction of it warms your bed at nights, because, by God, no self-respecting man ever will! And I'll see you in hell before I let you get your claws any deeper into my brother!'

She had listened, at first in uncomprehending hurt and a desperate understanding for how angry he was, but the unrelenting, unfair cruelty of his words whipped invisible lashes along her exposed skin, bringing her temper boiling to the surface. At the very last her brittle control snapped to pieces. She cried, her hands balled into fists at her sides, 'I don't want him, you stupid man! I never wanted him!'

'That's the most damning thing you have ever said about yourself!' he said violently, striding forward to grasp her by the shoulders in such a heavy iron grip that her body bowed underneath his strength. 'How dare you use people like so many pawns? How dare you play with their hearts?'

Blinded with the pain in her own aching heart, she raised up her hand to strike him, then stopped before his unflinching glare.

'No,' she said coldly, letting her hand fall open-palmed to her side again. 'I won't leave you the satisfaction of your so righteous wrath! I'll tell you the truth, and you can believe me or not as you please, though God knows your dogmatic presumptions probably won't let you! Yes, Joshua and I were going to say we were engaged— as a pretence, just to teach you a lesson for interfering in matters that didn't concern you!'

His mouth twisted bitterly. 'When did you concoct that cosy little set-up?'

'We decided the very day after you stormed into my life and called me names I wouldn't say to my worst enemy, let alone a total stranger!' she snapped, then told him, her eyes wide in astonishment at her own idiocy, 'Then I forgot about it—how do you like that? I just clean forgot, because I thought I got to know you, and I *thought* you were different from the man who h-hurt me by saying those awful things to my face!'

She gave a sharp, angry laugh, and her head bowed as the low sound turned into a gut-wrenching sob. His fingers tightened spasmodically on her shivering flesh; the look in his eyes was terrible. At that she came so near to breaking down and reaching for him that she wrenched out of his hold and took several quick strides away to face the print on his wall.

'Do you know what the real joke is?' she told him, as the tears spilled over and her shivering increased. 'Me. I'm the punch line. I was so sure that I wouldn't fall in love with any man! It just wasn't in the cards for me— I had other plans for my life. But you came along, and you did your damnedest to try to change my mind, and, fool that I am, I listened to you! Despite all my better judgement, I listened enough to consider changing my life for you, leaving my friends, home, school, everything. So there you have it, Matt. I got you, and you got me—and you tell me this. Which of us has won in the end? No——' this, when she sensed his uncontrolled movement behind her '—don't bother. You can claim the final trophy. I don't want it.'

'Sian,' Matt whispered hoarsely. 'God, Sian—listen to me——'

'No!' she cried, shrinking away as she felt his touch at the back of her head. 'I've listened to you and your fine talk too much already! Just go back to your own life, and leave me to mine!'

She whirled and rushed out of the room, and he raced after her, which so destroyed her sense of direction that she didn't watch where she was going and blundered straight into Jane's arms.

Of course, neither she nor Matt had heeded the level of their voices in the heat of the moment, and as a consequence had roused the whole household. So much for privacy, she thought, shaking like a leaf in the shelter of her friend's protective hold.

'Leave her be! Whatever you've done, now's not the time to correct it!' Jane said to Matt in a sharp, authoritative voice she had never heard before.

But Sian had seen Joshua, in the doorway of the guest bedroom looking as if he was facing an executioner, and her own private demon dragged her out of Jane's arms.

She strode over to him, white-faced and beyond restraint. 'What you did to me was bad enough. When you saw that things had changed between Matt and me, you should have come to me and we could have sorted it out. What you did to your own brother was unspeakable,' she said icily. 'It went far beyond a prank, Joshua. It was an act of malice done to someone who loves you, and that I find unforgivable. I don't know you. I thought I did, but I don't.'

Joshua looked stricken to his heart. Good, she thought in her own pain, good.

Something tugged. She looked around, unseeing, and let Jane lead her into Matt's bedroom. Then, fuelled by the glacier of ice that was crystallising over her bruised, overwrought emotions, she pulled away and stated flatly, 'I'm all right.'

'Well, you don't look it,' said Jane with unflattering bluntness.

Sian's head turned from side to side, then she strode for the door. Jane sprang for her. 'Where are you going?'

'To pack,' she snarled. 'I'm leaving as soon as I can get ready.'

'But where would you go?' the other girl exclaimed. 'What would you do?'

'I don't care!' she shouted, then leaned her elbows on the wall and put her head on her forearms. 'I'll go to the airport. I can take a bus from there to South Bend. I won't ride back in Joshua's car. I don't want to see him or talk to him.'

'Sian, it's half past one in the morning. You don't even know if the buses run at night. Could you just wait a minute and calm down, please?'

Sian raised her head and looked at the other girl in sizzling silence; she was wild to get away and only just able to keep from swearing at Jane out of love for her. Her friend stared, wide-eyed, then said quietly, 'Please. Five minutes. Then, if you insist, I'll get dressed and come with you.'

But she had halted in her impetuous path and reason had crept in. She closed her eyes; had she ever deserved such a friend as this? 'No, you're right,' she said, and sagged. 'I won't drag you out in the middle of the night. We can leave first thing in the morning.'

Matt's bed was quite big enough, so she shared it with Jane, and lay awake through what remained of the night, her head aching with the irony of it. Just after dawn, she rose and woke the other girl, then went to the study to drag on her last change of clothes. She slipped on a pair of sandals, stuffed her other things into her case, and felt the tears well up again.

In an excess of bad temper, she kicked the case across the room. No more tears. She had to be strong and keep her anger cold and hard. To allow warmth to creep back in now was to weaken; she had crept out of her self-imposed shell and found the wide world a hurting place to be, so she'd just crawl back to where she came from. Never mind that the shell seemed a small and confining prison. She could learn all over again how to take pride in being alone. It was only what her father had taught her, after all.

'Sian,' said Matthew from behind her.

She gasped, and whirled around, and cried, 'Get out!'

'No,' he said, his eyes dark and shadowed with sleeplessness. In the clear light his face had settled into hard and haggard lines. 'If I leave you now, you'll retreat forever behind your barriers and never come out again. I told you yesterday that I wanted you so badly I could hardly see straight. Remember?'

'Well,' she said with a bitter laugh, 'didn't we learn differently? You're too quick to anger, and I'm the credulous fool. So what? Better to learn it now, than later. Now, where's Jane? If she's coming with me, she'd better do it fast, because I'm not waiting around for any more of this post-mortem.'

With a muffled oath, he lifted his hands to rake through his hair distractedly, looking like a man who had come to the end of his tether. He said tightly, 'I am trying to tell you that I'm sorry! I behaved like an utter fool. I was angry, and hurt too, and lost control at the thought of you in Joshua's arms, or any other man's for that matter—can't you understand that?'

By luck he had managed to say the one thing that provoked the memory from last night of her own in-stinctive whiplash of reaction at the thought of him involved with another woman. Her furious desire to get away from him faded somewhat, and she looked at him with pained, very sad eyes.

'Oh, yes,' she sighed. 'I can. But just because you're ready for forgiveness, it doesn't mean that I'm ready to forgive you. And even if I did, today only shows how destructive we can be to each other.'

'But we weren't destructive last night until the very end,' he said quietly as he raised his head. 'We were good, and hopeful, and beginning to build something full of promise.'

'And it blew up in our faces,' she muttered, her face averted.

He replied, with pain and clarity, 'Everything that's ever been bad between us has been a misunderstanding; we seem to do pretty well at understanding. Don't you remember that as well, or are you so determined to block out everything about me?'

She shook her head helplessly at that, and he paused. She knew she was hurting him by her rejecting manner. He showed that transparently, but she didn't know if she could let go of the hard knot that lay like a coiled snake in her breast.

'Listen to reason for one moment,' he went on carefully, 'and try to hear it in spite of the fact that it comes from me. Yesterday you felt an entire world away from what you feel today. Who's to say that tomorrow you might not feel differently again? Let's give each other time to calm down, and look around us. Maybe things will look better, maybe not. I know I need to do some heavy thinking about faith and courtesy. Can we at least promise to talk to each other in a few days, without anger? Can we at least make that one, small step, even if it is to say goodbye?'

She closed her eyes, for she didn't know where to look. Oh, didn't she just warn herself a few minutes ago? To allow warmth to creep in was to weaken, and to hesitate was fatal.

'Just one phone call?' she said doubtfully.

'Hi, how are you? Have you been busy? I've missed you,' he responded immediately, with a tenderness in the words that looked fair to break her heart. It certainly cracked something, if only the brittle casing of an old, outworn shell. 'You know the sort of thing Just wait and see, it'll be easy.'

'I must be more of a fool than I thought,' she whispered, and looked up with wide, wet eyes.

He turned away, so that she could not see his face. 'Fine,' he said. How did he manage such calm? 'I'll call you Tuesday or Wednesday, all right?'

'A-all right.'

'I'm ready to go to the bus station whenever you are, Sian,' said Jane, her gaze very gentle as she looked at Matt's expression. 'Steven will go back to South Bend with Joshua.'

She cleared her throat. 'Then I guess we'd better go.'

She left without a backward glance, unable to trust her own precarious control or to fully believe in the new fragile tendrils of communication Matt had worked so hard to re-establish after their explosive confrontation.

The very stability in Jane's loyal, unquestioning friendship brought a hard lump to her throat as she stared out of the window on the bus ride back to South Bend. Jane talked, but in a soothing, placid voice about inessential matters that did not require a response, and after a time she could muster up enough energy to reply with some semblance of normality.

But underneath the murmur of undemanding conversation she realised that at least one question had been raised and answered by the weekend. She knew without a doubt that she had indeed fallen in love with Matt, and had even, in the midst of her pain and anger, found the courage to confess as much to his face. Otherwise his judgemental accusations could not have hurt her so badly, and she would never have agreed to even talking to him over the phone afterwards; she would have just broken off all contact and counted herself well rid of the whole affair.

As it was, she couldn't. Even at the height of her most uncontrollably damaging fury, he had managed to reach past the red cloud of pain and anger and touch her again in her soft, sensitive core. That he could do as much so quickly after his own heedless outburst of temper spoke, if nothing else, of his immediate remorse, and his own deep-seated uncertainty, and the desperate speed of man working very hard to recover fast from an unexpected, terrible blow.

Did that mean he loved her as well? She honestly couldn't tell. It might mean merely that he had outraged his own sense of fair judgement, and was appalled enough to try to make amends. He might decide that he couldn't bring himself to trust her as much as he thought he could, especially after learning of that stupid pretend engagement she had cooked up with Joshua, and his phone call in a few days would indeed be to say goodbye.

All she could do was wait, helplessly, trapped by her own emotions, a victim of her own fears and the aftermath of stress. She couldn't eat or sleep that Sunday evening, for fretting over what had happened, what she had said, what she should have said, and what might possibly come. She grieved for the breakdown of the beginning, yearned with an awesome loneliness for the comfort of his strong arms, and worried over what she would do or say to him when he phoned her.

But even in her most wild imagining, she couldn't have foreseen what would happen, or that the phone conversation that had assumed so much importance in her mind would never take place.

Jane left Monday morning to go to work. Sian showered and washed her hair, and sat at the kitchen table listlessly combing through the tangles when the front doorbell rang and she went to answer it.

Joshua stood on the doorstep, looking as drawn as she felt, and very much ashamed. Her mouth tightened as she stared at him, and her fingers clenched on the doorknob before she stepped back and gestured in abrupt silence for him to enter.

He went to the living-room, then turned around to face her. 'Sian, I'm sorry,' he said without preamble. 'I'm just so sorry.'

After all that had happened, and now this. It never rained, but it poured. She shook her head at the pleading in his face, sighed heavily and tightened the belt of her wrap. 'Why did you do it, Joshua? Couldn't you see that you would hurt us both? And Matt, especially Matt—he never explodes like he did, unless he's thoroughly shaken and upset. I can see that, now that I've had a chance to calm down.'

'You're right,' he said miserably. 'There's no excuse for what I did. I can't really even explain it very well. I was just so *jealous*. I saw you with him, and then everything went red. Matt always gets the best of everything, in career, lifestyle, friends, and it looked as if he would get you as well. I loved you.'

'You didn't love me,' she said quietly, turning back to face him. 'You were just infatuated and we both knew it.'

'No,' he said, just as quietly, with an honesty so painful it brought an ache to her already overburdened heart. 'I did love you, and I still do. Maybe it isn't quite the love I had imagined it was, but you were my friend first, and then he came along and seemed to take you away. Oh, I know it sounds possessive and ridiculous, but—Sian, you and the others have been some of the best things that ever happened to me. For the first time in my life I didn't feel like I came second to my big brother, who was always better, stronger and more popular than I could ever be. Don't you see? I thought I was losing you, and now, because of my own thoughtless, stupid actions, I probably have.'

She was unable to speak. Weren't they all to blame in some measure for what had happened? Didn't she, too, bear the guilt of her own irresponsible actions, for if she hadn't been so hell-bent on revenge she never would have taken things as far as they had gone.

'Anyway,' he said heavily, misreading her silence. 'I just thought I'd tell you—I've talked to Matt and explained everything. He's still angry but at least he understands now. And I just want to say again how sorry I am. I can't make it up to you, but I hope some day you can forgive me.'

'Oh, Joshua,' she sighed, and stepped forward to hold open her arms. He came to her in a rush and hugged her tight, and she said into his shirt, 'You fool. You silly fool, how could you think that our friendship would end just because I got involved with your brother?'

'I told you it sounded stupid!' he said with self-directed anger. 'Please—please don't let what happened come between us. My friends are the best and most important part of me.'

'I'll be your friend,' she whispered. 'Don't you see? I need you too. Just don't ever do anything like that to me again. I'm not big enough to forgive that much a second time.'

'Never, I promise.'

The moment was shattered as the doorbell rang again. Sian stepped away from Joshua and threw up her hands in disgust, while he wiped his face and found an unsteady laugh for the expression on her face. She went to answer it, smiling as she threw open the door, and, at the sight of the man standing on the porch step, everything stopped in her heart.

Malcolm, her father's friend and associate for over twenty years; Malcolm, whom she loved like an uncle and trusted implicitly. He was one of the few stolid anchors of stability in her young and changeable life. He never came to South Bend when her father visited her, to spare Sian the necessity of explaining Malcolm's presence to her friends. For years, the three of them had kept up the pretence that Sian hadn't guessed that Malcolm really worked as her father's bodyguard.

One look at his serious face, and she knew at once that something terrible had happened to her father.

'Sian is everything all right?' Joshua came into the hall. Neither she nor the silent man on the doorstep paid any heed to him.

She whispered, stricken, 'Is it bad?'

'Aye, lassie,' said Malcolm, and she moved like a sleepwalker into his great, bear-like arms. 'Can you come right away?'

'Of—of course. Let me throw some things into a bag and get my passport.'

She turned away, and her face was so dreadful that Joshua bridled and said aggressively to the stranger who had done this to her, 'Look here, who are you, and what do you want?'

'That's not for me to say, young man,' replied Malcolm quietly.

'Leave him alone, Joshua,' said Sian sharply, as panic rushed into fill the empty void in her mind. 'Look—could you write a note to Jane for me? Tell her I'll call just as soon as I can.'

'Sure,' he agreed readily, but she was striding down the hall even as he said it. He came with her, asking in helpless concern, 'Isn't there anything else I can do?'

She glanced at him as if from an immeasurable distance, this earnest and inexperienced young man who came from such a normal existence, and she said with quiet fatalism, 'I doubt there's anything anyone can do.'

CHAPTER TEN

AFTER the heat of the American Midwest, London seemed chilly and comfortlessly damp, as a mammoth bank of storm clouds moved north from Europe and enshrouded Britain.

The trip from South Bend to Heathrow was a nightmarish marathon. She and Malcolm took a flight from the Michiana Regional Airport to Chicago, then flew stand-by on the first available seats to London. Looking around her at the crowded, impersonal expanse of the O'Hare airport as they waited, Sian felt as though she had entered a world that was bleached of all colour and sound, as the quiet tired burr of Malcolm's voice explained in her ear just what had happened to her father.

That there had always been an element of risk to Devin's life was something that she'd had to accept over the passing years. He travelled light and fast, often with huge sums of cash and leaving behind irate casino owners, some of whom were unscrupulous characters who operated illegal establishments in the shadowy half-light existence of a global black market.

Despite Malcolm's cautionary admonitions, Devin had gained entrance to one particular gambling den just a few weeks ago and walked out again with a cool half-million in English pounds sterling. He had played and won against the owner himself, who was a man notorious for his gambling addiction, among other vices, and it was this man who had engineered an ambush just two nights ago.

Malcolm and Devin had managed to overcome the attackers, who had subsequently been arrested and were
now in prison on charges of attempted murder, but in
the process of the struggle Devin had been seriously
injured.

Reeling with exhaustion and distress, she nevertheless
rejected Malcolm's concerned suggestion that they go
back to the hotel suite that he'd booked for her under
an assumed name, and instead took a taxi straight from
Heathrow for the private hospital where Devin was.

A phone call had assured them that her father was
still alive, but in a coma from the head wound he had
sustained, and during the long ride in the taxi Sian had
cause to recall the quiet conversation she'd had with
Matthew only a week ago...

'You must have been a beautiful little girl. If I had a
daughter like that, it would break my heart to send her
away.'

'Would it?'

'Yes. I also know that if I were in a job or lifestyle
that was unsafe or unsuitable for that precious little girl,
I would send her away, to some place where she could
grow up safe, and I would deny myself the selfish
pleasure of letting her depend on me too much.'

So much fell into place, now that she could look back
with the clarity of hindsight. Devin's phone call to her,
his odd manner of behaving, his refusal to come to her
commencement and birthday party—they had been right
after the big score; of course he would never come within
a thousand miles of her if he thought for any reason he
was under threat. He wouldn't want any breath of danger
to fall on to her.

She leaned her forehead against the cold window-pane
of the taxi and sobbed drily, 'Oh, why did he do it,

Malcolm? He'd already made more than enough money to keep him in luxury for the rest of his life! He always knew how to quit when he was ahead. Why couldn't he have stopped all this years ago?'

'He didna want to, lassie,' said Malcolm quietly, his Scots burr becoming pronounced whenever he was under stress. 'Ever since your ma died, I think Devin's been lookin' fer some way to join her. He loved her, you know, more than anything, even enough to try to quit when they married. But his old life wouldna let go of him— too many people knew him, and there was always somebody looking to pay him back for winning too much. In the end, he left her, and you, for he wouldna ever have forgiven himself if something had happened to either of you because of him.'

Sian turned around to stare at Malcolm with wide, unseeing eyes, and her heart was just not big enough to sustain the huge grief that she felt. Was it that simple? Was that the final truth after so many years, when all her life she had believed her father to be a faithless, ir-responsible charmer? How could she have been so blind, for so long?

It wasn't any wonder that she had believed time and again how much Devin loved her, for that was the reality, not the number of times he had shrugged out of so many important events in her life. And she had grieved and convinced herself that his absence meant that he didn't care, when he had been protecting her the entire time.

'Why didn't he tell me?' she groaned.

'Sure, and put all that burden on a wee little lassie such as yourself?' replied Malcolm, shaking his greying head. 'No, Sian. That wouldna be right.'

There had been no change in Devin's condition when Sian and Malcolm reached the hospital. No, the doctors did not know whether he would come out of the coma or not; only time would tell them if he would survive. All they could do was wait.

Sian took up a vigil at Devin's bedside, and, watching the smooth, handsome planes of his serene face, she felt as if she were looking at a stranger. The man she had thought she had known all her life was gone, vanished in an insubstantial puff of air, and she was terrified to think she might never come to know the real flesh-and-blood person before her.

Time meant nothing. Food was put in front of her and taken away again unnoticed. She dozed in the chair where she sat, and left the hospital only to wash and change into the new clothes Malcolm went to buy for her. Any more danger from an outside source, the police had assured her, was highly unlikely. Malcolm kept vigil with her, and she was grateful enough for his affection and loyalty, but she had never felt so lonely in her entire life.

She needed someone to hold her, and reassure her that everything would somehow work out all right, for her faith and stamina were draining away bit by bit with the hours that trickled by. She needed someone to be strong for her, and reliable, someone whose shoulder she could rest her tired head on. Oh, God, how she needed Matthew, but he was half a world and an entire lifestyle away, and Sian had lost all capacity for hope.

At last persuaded that Devin was not about to die in her absence, she left her father's side on Thursday afternoon to phone the States, planning the time difference so that she would catch Jane before she went to work. At the sound of her friend's voice at the other end of the connection, she nearly broke down and cried.

She explained what had happened, as briefly and concisely as she could, and when the dreadful words had dried out in her tight throat Jane exclaimed, 'Oh, Sian! We've been so worried about you! It was all just so terrible, you vanishing into thin air like that—I've been beside myself with fear, but I never imagined anything like that could have happened! Matt went crazy when you disappeared. He came out to South Bend after he'd called on Tuesday and you weren't here.'

Her heart leaped so violently she felt it as a physical pain, and she gripped the phone receiver so hard her fingers went numb. 'Is he there now?'

She knew the answer in the hesitation in her friend's voice, even more when Jane said very gently, 'No, darling. He's gone back to Chicago. He said that he had too many responsibilities to put them on hold until you decided to show up. But I'm sure that as soon as he knows why you went away the way you did, everything will get sorted out somehow...Sian? Sian, are you there?'

She never heard Jane. Too much had happened to her in the last few days, and the long unrelenting crisis on her mind and body at last took its toll. A crushing weight of darkness had descended on to her shoulders, and the phone receiver slipped out of her nerveless hand to fall dangling from its cords. Always running away, aren't you? echoed the accusing ghost in her head. And you weren't there when I called, even though you promised.

Guess what, kiddo? Looks like you're going to lose this game of Solitaire, all hands down.

It was a long fall to the ground, without Matthew's arms to catch her.

*   *   *

She woke gradually, and lay for some time blinking up at a strange ceiling. She was in a large bed and she couldn't remember how she had come to be there. But she remembered the dream of Paris in the spring-time, with the rain falling softly on her upturned cheeks, and, as she heard the shadow of movement on the other side of a half-open door, she stirred groggily and murmured, 'Matt?'

Quick footsteps sounded outside, and a shadow fell across her body from the indirect illumination. 'Lassie?' said Malcolm quietly. The first tentative gladness in her heart withered away as dark reality slammed home. She turned her face away with a silent sob; of course, now she remembered. Of course Matt wasn't there.

'What happened?' she croaked out.

'You fainted.' Malcolm came into the room, sat on the edge of the bed and laid cool, dry fingers against her cheek.

'Good God,' she exclaimed weakly. 'I didn't know I had it in me.'

It was a feeble attempt and Malcolm wasn't smiling. 'The doctors said it was just exhaustion. I warned you that you were pushing yourself too hard, but you're just like your da. You wouldna listen.'

'How is he?' Impelled by a renewed sense of urgency, she pushed herself to her elbows, cursing and amazed at the trembling in her limbs.

'No change. I'm sorry, lassie—now wait just a bloody minute! You're not getting out of that bed until you've had a bite to eat! You've slept round the clock. You need food in your stomach or you'll just faint again. The hospital will call if there's any news.'

Despite her irritable complaints, Malcolm ordered up a hot nourishing meal from room service and stood over her until she had forced down enough food to satisfy him. Only then would he let her rise, and as she showered and dressed in jeans and a blouse she had to admit that, if nothing else, at least she felt steadier on her feet.

The heavy cloud cover had broken while she slept, and the Friday evening sunset was a rainbow kaleidoscope as she and Malcolm left the hotel. With a wince she fumbled in her purse for her sunglasses, for her dry, strained eyes could not take the shining brilliance. When their taxi had dropped them off at the main entrance of the hospital, Malcolm put a massive arm around her shoulders and led her inside, his searching gaze scouring the immediate vicinity.

Observing the protective attitude, Sian said drily, 'I thought any more danger wasn't likely.'

'Aye, well, it doesna hurt to be careful, lassie,' he said, his soothing tones at complete odds with the tough, capable stance of his body as he pushed open the door for her to enter. 'Especially with your da already occupying one hospital bed.'

She stepped inside as she argued, 'But surely since the men who attacked you have confessed, and Scotland Yard has the casino owner in custody, there isn't anything more to worry about?'

They were passing through the information desk and main lounge, which due to the evening visiting hours, was crowded with people.

A man rose to his feet to walk towards them. 'Sian?'

Her head started to turn automatically, in profound surprise and the first, incredible start of recognition at the familiarity of the deep, husky voice. But all she saw of him was a blur, for she was shoved violently against the wall as Malcolm said sharply, 'Look out!'

She reeled into the wall, then recovered with desperate speed. Malcolm was spinning with lethal grace to thwart the advance of the intruder. Before conscious thought had time to register, she flung herself bodily between the two men. 'No, Malcolm!'

Malcolm's fist had already lifted into a swing. Even as he tried to throw his weight back, he was caught off balance and the blow would have connected with stunning force into the side of her face, except that the newcomer thrust out a powerful forearm with lightning speed to cover her vulnerable, exposed head.

The two men stared at each other over Sian, both pale and shaken, for had the blow connected it would have broken her jaw. She never realised how close she had come to injury. She had twisted under the canopy of their outstretched arms to stare at the newcomer and whispered unbelievingly, 'Matt?'

His hazel eyes dropped to her, and he looked hard, haggard, and gloriously real, and then his face softened with indescribable tenderness as he said huskily, 'Oh, love, I came as soon as I heard.'

She took a sleep-walker's step forward. He reached to gather her hungrily to him, and the urgent strength of his hold was such sustenance to her starving soul that she clung to his neck.

She felt as if her heart had leapt right out of her skin. It resided in the large, solid frame of the man who bowed himself around her, beating in time with his own. He cupped the back of her head, pulled her face to him and drove into her mouth with shaking ferocity.

Tears slipped out of the corners of her eyes and streaked their salted path downwards. Very carefully Matt lifted the dark glasses away from her face. At the sight of the heavy shadows ringing the delicate skin around her eyes, her beauty bruised by the events of the past week, his own gaze darkened with acute pain.

'But how did you know where to find me?' she asked, touching his lean cheek with wondering fingers, for she still could not quite bring herself to believe that he was actually with her and not a figment of her imagination.

'Jane,' he said harshly. 'She called me right after you talked to her. Remember, you told her which hospital your father was in. I packed my bag and was at the airport inside of forty-five minutes. Luckily there was a last-minute cancellation on a British Airways flight, otherwise I might still be going insane at O'Hare. When I got into Heathrow this morning, I called around at every hotel in the phone books, but you weren't anywhere to be found, so I came here to wait.'

'Malcolm booked me in a suite at the Hilton under an assumed name,' she told him in bemusement.

His expression hardened, and his hold around her waist tightened so that her breath whistled in her throat.

'Yes,' he said, his voice a grim, graceless scrape of sound. 'Jane said that your father had been attacked. My God. I've been in seven different kinds of hell these past few days! First Joshua told me how you went white as a sheet when some strange man showed up on your doorstep, and you just meekly went away with him without a word of explanation. I've been torturing myself ever since with all kinds of scenarios, each one more wild and outlandish than the last. The only thing I could think of was that he had some kind of Svengalian hold on you, and that I would never see you again.'

'It was Malcolm. He's my father's associate,' she said, shocked by the flash of remembered terror that twisted his expression. 'He never came to South Bend. Whenever my father visited me, he was alone. I think he wanted to appear ordinary—as much like everyone else's parents as possible. When Malcolm showed up without Daddy, I knew something terrible had happened. All I could think of was that my father might die before I saw him again.'

'How is he?' he asked quietly.

She bowed her head against him and shuddered. 'In a coma. Malcolm and Daddy tried their best, but there were three of them—one of his attackers struck him over the head with an iron pipe.'

'God,' he muttered, running his strong fingers through her hair, as if to reassure himself that she was whole and unscathed. 'No wonder that fellow had such a hair-trigger reaction when I walked up to you.'

'Oh, Matt,' she groaned, 'he looks so white, just like a wax image—I don't know what I would do if he died— he's the only family I've got——'

'No, oh, no.' He breathed the words, almost crooning, into the shell of her ear, cradling and soothing her with every giving part of him. 'Sian, no matter what else happens, you'll always have me.'

It took a moment for what he said to sink in. When it did, it was only what she could have wished for, but Sian's personal demon did not always listen to the dictates of her heart.

It said bitterly, in her voice, 'Just as I had you over the weekend?'

He stiffened and drew back, his own swift anger flashing in those predator's eyes, and his hands, sliding to her shoulders, became claws. He shook her, not once or consciously or hard, but in a fine continuous tremor, and what it communicated to her in terms of his depth of emotion and endurance was a corner-stone revelation. She stared, transfixed, at his face.

'Yes,' said Matthew starkly. 'As you had me over the weekend. Giddy, aroused, terrified, amazed, humbled. In hell. As you had me from the very first moment I laid eyes on you. I came to your party with everything planned, how I would approach you, what I would say. It was to be such a reasonable conversation. I stood on your back porch, and looked across the yard at you, and everything sane and sensible blew up in my head. You were the most desirable woman I had ever seen, and you were, as I thought then, engaged to be married to my brother. God in heaven, you belonged to another man, and I went crazy. I was terrified that I might have come into your life too late.'

'Matthew——' she whispered, in awe and pity. She raised her hands to stroke his transformed expression, to check the terrible beauty of his words, but he was ungovernable.

'I love you,' he said from the back of his throat. 'I love you in a way that has redefined the course of my life. I love you more than anything else in the world, as if I've never known the meaning of the word before—I couldn't stay away from you any more than I could stop breathing. I thought the ache I felt for you was like nothing I'd ever experienced, but it was nothing compared to the agony I went through when I realised you might be in danger yourself, while I was stuck in a soulless airport three thousand miles away. I only hope to God I never have to go through that again.'

'Stop,' she breathed, touching him, straining towards him. 'Oh, darling, stop.'

His introspective gaze focused on her with sharp, ravenous clarity. 'Never,' he told her quietly.

If before she thought she was starving, now her heart felt full to bursting. She closed her eyes and exclaimed,

'You've made me so angry. I've never been so furious as I have been with you. You shot straight through all my defences as if they never existed, and from that first moment onwards I seemed to spend every waking moment thinking of you, swearing at you, yearning for you, denying you. I thought I knew what I wanted out of life, and I was so smug and self-satisfied with my plans—then you came along and, with hardly any effort at all, you showed me how all those things I wanted—stability, a proper home and family—were only reflections of the love I felt for you.'

'That wasn't effortless,' said Matthew with a twisted smile, and a new-born light in his eyes that warmed her to the depths of her soul. 'I worked as I've never worked before, trying to convince you in as many ways as I possibly could how good we could be for each other. I set out to seduce you, not just physically, but intellectually and emotionally as well, holding my breath every time you backed away, and wincing inside every time I put my foot wrong. I felt so desperate after the first few days, I was reduced to inviting all your friends to my place for the weekend, and, when it looked as if you were the only one who wasn't coming, I felt a king-sized fool.'

'You never showed it,' she said drily. 'You were so cool, so contained.'

He tilted back her chin and let his intent, heavy-lidded gaze fall to her lips. 'Oh, no?' he murmured. 'I seem to recall a certain scene played in a restaurant parking lot, and the follow-up scenario in your kitchen. I couldn't keep my hands off you! I was a moth to a flame, circling you, beating against you, singeing my wings and dying from it.'

A dark wave of red colour stained the pale skin covering her cheekbones as a flicker of remembered passion licked through her body. He laughed, a slumbrous, smoky, satisfied sound.

She looked about them, embarrassed for the exposure and vulnerability she felt, but nobody paid them any attention. Emotional scenes in a hospital were everyday occurances, and Malcolm, bless his soul, had disappeared discreetly some time ago.

Matt had sobered at once, and with a dark, sombre look he said quietly, 'Last Saturday, I felt on top of the world. You came to me, and kissed me, and set my soul on fire. With every reason to hope, I went to talk to Joshua, and he pulled the rug out from underneath my feet. Sian, I can never tell you how sorry I am for those things I said to you. I was out of control, and wild with the thought that you weren't as caught up with me as I was with you. I regretted it almost immediately, but I couldn't snatch the words out of the air. They hung there, between us, and then, when you'd confessed how close you had come to loving me, I knew that I'd cut my own throat with my wilful anger.'

'But I didn't just come close,' she said, her green eyes wide and fixed on his. 'I did love you, and I do love you. I never needed anyone as much as I needed you in these last few days, and I've been so lonely and scared——'

'Oh, darling,' he groaned, and bent to kiss her with slow fervency, and the calibre of feeling in his caress was so deep that it swept away any remaining cobweb of doubt in her mind.

'I'm so glad you came!' she whispered against his warm mouth.

He sighed, and drank her words in with open lips. 'I'll always come. I'll always be here right beside you, always. No matter what.'

'But what about your work?' she asked, pulling back to stare at him worriedly. 'You've got so many people depending on you, I'll understand if you have to go back. I'm just happy you managed to come at all, and—well, there's no telling how long I'll have to stay.'

It hurt her deeply to say it: to admit in words that Devin's condition was so unknown, to free Matthew from any sense of obligation when all she wanted to do was to cling shamelessly and beg him to stay.

Matt's head raised and he said shortly, with a savage frown, 'You must be joking. Do you honestly think I'd leave, with your father in hospital, and God knows what kind of danger you might be in?'

'But there isn't any danger!' she exclaimed. 'Honestly.'

He looked at her in frank disbelief and replied coolly, 'Your father's friend certainly thought otherwise.'

Sian waved an impatient hand. 'Malcolm's been under a lot of strain. He blames himself for what happened to my father, but the people responsible are already in gaol. You don't have to worry about me.'

'If it's all right with you,' he said drily, 'I think I'll find that out for myself, thank you very much. And as far as my work is concerned, there's nothing I left that can't be taken care of when I get back. No, Sian—you can't put up any more barriers between us. Life's too short for that. By the grace of God, and despite our own idiotic behaviour, we've managed to find each other, and we'll just have to rearrange our own lives accordingly, because now that I've got you, I'm not going to let go again. Ever. You're looking in the face of a lifetime sentence, so tough luck.'

'I'm just going to have to learn how to handle it?' she asked, her eyes alight with memory and laughter.

His impatience melted away into a sexy grin. 'You got it.'

'Lassie!' Malcolm's urgent shout from down the corridor made her jump violently, and stark fear bleached away all signs of the growing happiness that had sweetened her face. She and Matt looked at each other for one grim moment, then she turned and nearly fell to the floor in weak relief at the sight of the beaming smile on Malcolm's face. 'It's yer da—he's awake and asking for you!'

'Matt!' she turned to him with a smile of such blinding loveliness that his breath caught in his throat.

He whirled her around and grabbed hold of her hand. 'Come on!'

They ran swiftly through the corridors, and people turned to look, and nurses frowned, but nothing could eclipse the huge perfection of the joy that washed over her in waves so tangible that it was nearly visible light.

She pointed the direction out to Matt, and he thrust open the door for her to rush through. At the sight of Devin's clear, lucid gaze, she smiled and cried at once. She came up to his bedside to take his hand tenderly, and she said, 'Oh, Daddy. I've been so worried. How do you feel?'

'Sure, and how else do you expect me to feel?' said Devin with a weak grin, as his eyes lit up with love. 'Like I've lost an argument with a brick, of course. And don't you go scolding me, mind. I know I've been a stubborn fool.'

'I'll scold you if I want. Don't you ever, ever do that to me again!' she said, but gently, as she stroked his hand.

'No, lass,' he said meekly, then he caught sight of Matt standing silently behind her. 'What's this? And here you've been telling me there's no man in your life.'

'There is now,' said Matt as she opened her mouth. His hand settled on to her shoulder.

'Sure, and now he'll be expecting me to play the stern father, and here I am with my head wrapped up like an Indian prince,' said Devin with a dubious scowl, to which she laughed. 'And just what are your intentions towards the most beautiful lassie you're ever likely to see, me young lad?'

'Strictly honourable,' said Matthew, who then added, 'And far too explicit to be telling her father on his sick-bed.'

At that, he surprised Devin into laughing so hard that Sian grew alarmed and leaned over him. 'Aye, darling,' said her father complacently when he could catch his breath. 'It looks like you've caught yourself a live one.'

Matt's firm fingers tightened on her shoulder, running threads of sensual warmth and promise throughout her body, and a vital, unspoken message of commitment. Of course he would always be there. Hadn't he wooed her from a different State and chased her across two countries and an ocean? She said with deceptive placidity, while a twinkle was born in her eye, 'Why, yes.'

She was thinking of a story her father had once told her, about the devil and an Irishman.

POSTCARDS FROM EUROPE

HARLEQUIN PRESENTS®

Travel across Europe in 1994 with Harlequin Presents. Collect a new *Postcards From Europe* title each month!

Don't miss
DARK SUNLIGHT
by Patricia Wilson
Harlequin Presents #1644

Available in April, wherever Harlequin Presents books are sold.

HPPFE4

Hi—

The sun was shining brightly here in Spain <u>until</u> I met Felipe de Santis. The man is used to giving orders and doesn't respect my abilities as a journalist. But I'm going to get my story—and I'm going to help Felipe's sister!

Love, Maggie

P.S. If only I could win Felipe's love....

Take 4 bestselling love stories FREE

Plus get a FREE surprise gift!

Special Limited-time Offer

Mail to Harlequin Reader Service®

3010 Walden Avenue
P.O. Box 1867
Buffalo, N.Y. 14269-1867

YES! Please send me 4 free Harlequin Presents® novels and my free surprise gift. Then send me 6 brand-new novels every month, which I will receive months before they appear in bookstores. Bill me at the low price of $2.44 each plus 25¢ delivery and applicable sales tax, if any*. That's the complete price and—compared to the cover prices of $2.99 each—quite a bargain! I understand that accepting the books and gift places me under no obligation ever to buy any books. I can always return a shipment and cancel at any time. Even if I never buy another book from Harlequin, the 4 free books and the surprise gift are mine to keep forever.

106 BPA ANRH

Name	(PLEASE PRINT)	
Address	Apt. No.	
City	State	Zip

This offer is limited to one order per household and not valid to present Harlequin Presents® subscribers. *Terms and prices are subject to change without notice. Sales tax applicable in N.Y.